BOARDWALK STORIES

ROSLYN BERNSTEIN

with photographs by DR. KENNETH S. TYDINGS

BLUE EFT PRESS

www.blueeftpress.com

info@blueeftpress.com

Text © 2009 by Roslyn Bernstein
All Photos © Estate of Dr. Kenneth S. Tydings

ISBN-13   978-0-9840546-0-2

Cover Photo by Dr. Kenneth S. Tydings

Printed in the United States of America

CONTENTS

❈

For my mother Bea

Digging to China

Summer 1951

WE WORE ALUMINUM DOG TAGS with our religion stamped on them, so that a stranger would know where to bury us after an atom bomb attack. It was the fifties, a time when televisions were just beginning to appear in the East End. We lived in the West End, near Our Lady of the Benevolent Sacred Heart Church, a wooden building with beige stucco walls and a stained glass window of Christ on the cross facing the Atlantic Ocean.

We were the outsiders, longing to belong, the only kids on the block who had never been inside the church, although we often stood by the heavy oak door peering in. Jewish girls didn't attend Sacred Heart Church and they most definitely did not go to the Sisters of Charity School.

Joanne and I lived on the same block and we ate lunch together every day at school, unwrapping the silver foil on our peanut butter and jelly sandwiches at a table far from the other girls. Her father, Arthur, was a lawyer who was proud to be an atheist. Her mother lit Friday night candles, but never went to synagogue.

My parents ate clam fritters on Friday night. They sent me to the neighborhood elementary school, where green paper Christmas trees adorned the classroom doors and where a torn blue and gold Chanukah menorah was taped carelessly in one corner. Joanne and I knew the words to "Silent Night" although our mothers forbad us from singing Jesus' name. Just mouth the lyrics, our mothers said. Never, never say them.

But I never listened. I sang "Silent Night" at the top of my voice, raising my volume when I came to the words, "Holy Infant So Tender and Mild." After all, it was forbidden. I envied Patricia Everson, the blonde girl who sat in front of me. She was always crossing herself. "Mary, Mother of God, have mercy on me," she said before she did every long division problem. "Lord Jesus help me," she whispered as she stood before the class and tried in vain to spell the names of the Indian tribes in New York State.

Joanne and I often talked about the bomb. She was sure that it would strike New England, where the Boston Tea Party had taken place.

"Boston is a more revolutionary place than New York," she told me, as we sat in the wet sand, looking for jingle shells. We had studied the American Revolution two years earlier. Now, we were deep into the Cold War and Communism. I was sure that Russia was going to drop a big bomb somewhere and that we would all disappear into a mushroom cloud of smoke.

She argued with me incessantly but there was no dissuading me from this grim vision. I read the newspapers that my father brought home every evening—The World Telegram, The Evening Sun, The Journal American. I'd sit on my front porch, swatting flies, and turning the pages.

My favorite was The Journal American, a paper that included a daily editorial on the woes of communism. "Listen to this, Joanne," I said one day as I pulled a scrap of newspaper from my beach bag and began reading the bold headline: "The Bomb is Ticking. Do You Hear It?"

Joanne shook her head. "Don't believe everything you read," she said. Her voice was loud and dramatic. I continued reading: "If we don't take any action, it will explode on our hallowed soil." "That means on our beach," I said. "Soil means sand."

"I'm not scared," she said. "It's all propaganda. They want us to be frightened."

I twisted my dog tag as she spoke, feeling the raised letter J for Jewish that was stamped above my name. Then, I crumpled the clipping into a ball and threw it into the water. It landed on the crest of a wave, and disappeared into the dark surf.

Russia was far away. Very cold. The people wore fur hats and thick coats that made them look fat. I had seen pictures of them, trudging down snowy streets. In America, we were warm and the sun was shining. We stretched out on the beach in striped canvas chairs, lathered in suntan oil.

Ten feet away from us, closer to the water, four girls were building sand cathedrals. It was a contest to see who could build the tallest one, with gargoyles that would scrape the clouds. The girls filled their pails with water, grabbed handfuls of sand and dripped the wet sand slowly through their small fingers. They moved from side to side, careful not to topple the delicate steeples. The oldest, Barbara, had just finished her second year of Catholic high school.

Thanks to the nuns, Barbara considered herself an expert on churches. I could hear every word she said. "In Europe, there are hundreds of cathedrals, with stained glass windows," she said. "Inside, they are so cold, that you have to wear a sweater in the summertime, and so dark you have to light candles to see."

Barbara always seemed to know what she was doing. She came from a good Catholic family, one of seven children. Her mother went to church every morning and sent all of her children to Catholic school, where the nuns hit your fingers with the metal edge of a ruler if you wrote with your left hand. You had to say your Rosary. Bow before the picture of the Pope. Wear your plaid jumper three inches below the knees. Never chew gum, which the girls did anyway, sticking it underneath the seats of their wooden desks when the nuns approached.

I knew them from my summers renting in the neighborhood, playing stickball on the narrow streets, and digging tunnels in the sand. One year ago, we had finally moved, fleeing Brooklyn and the only home that I had ever known, a red brick apartment building that smelled of cabbage, for a wooden bungalow near the beach. My father, Marvin, wanted to improve our lives, to fill our lungs with fresh air. For him, leaving the city was a step up, worth the two-hour commute each day by train

Joanne and I attended public school, two blocks from the brick Sisters of Charity building. Compared to their school, our school was old and worn. The windows were always in need of washing, and when the light hit the panes at the right angle, you could see hundreds of pieces of tape, the residue of art projects long since destroyed, clinging to the glass. The schoolyard was covered with a fine coating of sand, blown from the beach, and the seesaw needed a coat of paint.

One of the nuns swept their schoolyard early each morning. She was just finishing up when we passed and she would wave to us, as if to say, this is the proper way to do things. Tell that to your principal. But we didn't say a word. Our principal wouldn't have appreciated it. He had all he could do to keep us under control and to see to it that the cleaning staff emptied the garbage cans, filled with squashed milk containers from yesterday's lunch, and washed the linoleum floors in the lunchroom. Public school kids were an unruly lot, sent to stand in the corner for shooting straw wrappers or spitballs or rubber bands. We talked when we were supposed to be quiet and we wrote the answers to the spelling test questions on the inside of our palms.

None of the girls in the Sisters of Charity School would have dared to misbehave. Certainly not Barbara, who sat on the beach dripping tiny drops of sand onto her church steeples. Barbara understood self-control. If one of the girls interrupted her, she silenced her quickly and easily by raising her finger to her lips. Do not speak, the gesture said. Or else. She had learned it from the nuns.

"Light from the outside filtered in through the colored glass," Barbara said, as she resumed her description of the ancient cathedrals. "It struck the stone floor, making odd patterns. When you looked up, you saw the windows glowing: yellow, red, blue. Christ on the cross, the story of the crucifixion. The Virgin Mary."

The girls nodded as she spoke and then, after a moment's hesitation, crossed themselves. They could imagine the shining glass windows. There was a round, stained-glass window in Sacred Heart, above the main altar. The light from it bounced off a tall, silver chalice, landing magically on the head of the priest.

None of this made any sense to Joanne or me. They were busy building gothic drip cathedrals; we sat there obsessed with digging the deepest hole that we could dig, all the way to China. China was on the other side of the world, far from the West End. China was exotic, a land filled with bamboo. The West End was plain and familiar, a land filled with sand. If you dug hard and long enough, down, down through the coarse, wet sand, you could escape.

China was Communist, I said, but Joanne insisted that it was a good place. The workers ran the country. The leaders read books. Even farmers spouted wisdom. My father once told me that the Chinese expression for suffering was eating bitterness. There was nothing bitter about their food. Wonton soup with strips of pork lurking at the bottom of the white flowered bowl; crisp egg rolls, oily to the touch; lobster Cantonese, sauce streaked with egg white and reeking of garlic. We Jews loved Chinese food, more than we loved the foods we ate in the shtetl, gefilte fish and soup made of potato skins. Chinese food was worth digging to the other end of the earth for.

I imagined that when our tunnel was deep enough I would just slide down the shoot and land on a Chinese street, as shocked as Dorothy, whose house fell to the ground, landing her in Oz. Plop. Plop. Thud. Thud. I would hit the hard mud, rocking back and forth for a few moments, before I gained my balance. I would open my eyes to discover that I was surrounded by a crowd gaping at me in disbelief. Who was this girl who looked so strange? How white her skin was and how odd the shape of her eyes. Why was she dressed in such peculiar clothing, and how to explain the dark curly hair? The men stared at me. And the women and children, too. Even the babies, strapped to their mothers' breasts, stared without blinking.

We took turns digging. Joanne was stronger than I and she was fearless. When the hole became too deep to reach the bottom, she insisted that I lower her inside, holding on to her ankles as she scooped sand from the bottom. That was definitely too scary. None of this acrobatic upside-down stuff for me. I reached in as far as I could and grabbed a handful of sand. It was wetter and less fine. It felt like coarse salt, the kind of salt that came in a red cylindrical container marked kosher, the salt that my father's mother in Brooklyn sprinkled on her Friday-night chicken while we sat at our table in the West End picking fried bits of clams from our teeth.

Barbara and her friends attended the Sisters of Charity School across the street from the Church. It was filled with neighborhood girls, from junior high through high school, whose blue-collar Irish parents did not want their daughters to share classes with boys. There would be time to marry and have babies. Before that, there was to be no sex.

Most of the girls came from families of 10 or 12 children, crammed into the wooden frame houses by the beach. Their parents had migrated to the little bungalows in the 1930s and 40s, fleeing New York City. They stayed, one generation after another attending mass at Our Lady of the Benevolent Sacred Heart Church.

Their fathers were plumbers, carpenters, and truck drivers. Their mothers were full-time homemakers who sewed their daughters' First Communion dresses and volunteered at the Ladies' Auxiliary. Summers were spent on the beach, where they planted their beach chairs in the white sand, next to the renters, middle- and upper-middle class families from New York City, who bought their kids ice cream every day from the Good Humor truck and whose children wore bathing suits that matched their terry cloth beach shirts.

The kids in the West End passed their bathing suits from brother to brother and from sister to sister, no matter how stretched, torn, and faded. They were badges of honor, like the communion dresses and suits, with their starched white sashes and pristine white shirts, which were passed along from one generation to the next, or the two-wheelers, painted over so many times that their scratched rear fenders displayed all the colors of the rainbow.

Barbara stopped speaking to concentrate on the sand steeple. She was nearing its pinnacle, time to show her skill. One false move, one drop of sand too heavy, and the steeple soaring toward heaven would topple. She reached into the pail for a tiny globule of sand and let it drip downward, holding her breath. It landed on the top of the tower of drips. For a moment, the tower shook. Then, it was still.

She crossed herself in thanks and the other girls crossed themselves too. Joanne and I stopped digging and watched them, as they huddled in their tight circle. They knew who their God was. They were giving thanks to Jesus, the savior, Jesus the son of Mary, Jesus the Jew. Jesus hovered over their lives, blessing them at every moment—when they crossed the street and when their sand creation was in danger of falling.

We were almost at China now—at least we hoped we were. As we dug deeper, the sand became wetter and wetter. The bottom of the hole was fast filling up with water. My fingers were red from digging, coarse grains of sand under my fingernails.

Barbara reached into the pail again for one more globule of sand. The wind was getting a bit stronger and the tide was starting to come in. Wave after wave crashed against the sand, creeping closer and closer. The girls began their Hail Marys.

"Hail Mary, full of grace, the Lord is with thee; blessed art thou amongst women, and blessed is the fruit of thy womb, Jesus. Holy Mary, Mother of God, pray for us sinners, now and at the hour of our death. Amen."

I could not take my eyes off of them, these blue-eyed, freckle-faced, blonde-haired girls of the West End. Their voices were loud, interrupted only by the crashing surf. The waves licked the edges of the sand cathedral. They said their Hail Marys again, louder, more fervently. The wind gusted and a large swell of water formed, rising, like a wave during a full moon. The girls fled to the seaweed-covered jetty as the water rolled in. Suddenly, the wave crested and surged forward, crashing over their cathedral.

When the water retreated, seconds later, all that remained was a large mound of sand. There were no gargoyles. There were no gothic spires scraping the clouds. I stared at the mound for a moment, then reached down into the hole and continued digging to China.

Eavesdropping

March 1953

IT WAS EIGHT O'CLOCK ON A FRIDAY NIGHT. The dinner dishes were washed and stacked neatly in the dish rack. All that remained was the aluminum roasting pan, which was covered with burnt pieces of chicken skin and needed soaking. I followed my usual routine, filling the pan with hot, soapy water. Then, I sponged the Formica table and opened the screen door.

"Don't come home too late." It was my mother's voice, calling from a back bedroom. She knew where I was going—to Joanne's house, only four bungalows away. We lived one short block from the white, sandy beach that meets the Atlantic.

This was the poor side of town, home to blue-collar Irish and Italians and a few misfit Jews, either too cheap or too poor to live in the stucco houses with tile roofs that lined the streets of the East End. Most of the houses were single-story, with garages on the street level and large front porches. They stood ten feet apart, their side entries almost touching. Several of the houses, like my own, were two stories high, with the second-floor apartment rented out for income.

I was 16 years old, a junior in high school, a red brick building located a little over a mile from my home. I had been living in the West End for two years now, after several summers renting a small bungalow with my parents. My father, Marvin, who long ago abandoned his birth name Menachem, never went to college, having immigrated to New York City at the age of 12. As the youngest in his family, he was the only one who graduated from high school, attending evening classes where, because he was smart, he was promoted from third grade to high school in eight months. Days were spent working in a retail store, squeezing toes into shoes that were too small for them. "I never met a woman who said that she wore a size 10," he always told me.

Dad was a dreamer but he knew that dreams didn't earn you a living. So, he settled for a job in the City Budget Office, using his talent for numbers to work his way up the civil service ladder. He loved books and he was determined that his daughter would be the most brilliant, the best educated, the most cultured kid in her class. Boy, did that put a burden on me.

Their fathers were carpenters and plumbers, bartenders and truck drivers—big, burly men who drank too much beer at the local bar. They'd wave when I passed by.

"Smarty," they cried out in booming voices that you could hear all the way down the street. "Hey, smarty, how are ya doing?"

I'd never answer them. My father said that I should ignore their catcalls. "They're jealous," he said. I was not so sure. Their kids beat me up on Halloween, sacked me with flour, and drenched me with water. They'd whistle for their dogs and chase me down the block.

I learned to stay away, spending my time after school in the local library, where I did my homework and read straight through the orange biography series on famous Americans, from Abigail Adams to John Peter Zenger. In one year, I read all 215 biographies. Every evening, after dinner, I gave my dad a little report. He loved to hear me tell the stories of people who triumphed over poverty, of Americans who became famous. "You will too," he said.

The library reading room was usually empty, except for a half dozen old women who slept with their heads on the tables, worn shopping bags at their feet. This year, I am in love with Marie Curie, that strange, brilliant woman who won two Nobel Prizes, one in physics and one in chemistry. I have abandoned my dream of becoming a ballerina, Alicia Markova in a white tutu, en pointe, for life as a white-coated physicist in a laboratory. I am in love with photons and electrons.

On the weekends I'd go to Joanne's house. She was my age although we were not in the same class. Joanne had thin, blonde hair and thick glasses, like her mother. Her house was shabby—newspapers lying on the floor and holes in the slipcovers, which were very much in need of washing. Strangers came and went there, foreigners who spoke different languages and smoked cigars. Most of the guests were men with dark beards.

Even when Joanne was not home, I would sit in her living room, fascinated by the conversation. No one asked me to leave. I plopped myself down on a chair in the corner and watched and listened. I had come to recognize the visitors. Eduardo, from British Honduras, was there almost every Friday night. He arrived with George and Henry, all three of them carrying bags of newspapers. Joanne's mother always served coffee and they sat at the big square table discussing the news. They were angry with President Eisenhower.

"A great general, perhaps," Eduardo said, "but a weak and foolish president."

"Not a leader like Stalin," Henry said. "We will never be able to replace him."

Stalin had died two days earlier. I read the story in The World Telegram & Sun, the newspaper that my father brought home every evening.

George loved Stalin too. "I met him once," George said, "in Moscow."

I was intrigued. How and why had George traveled to Moscow?

One Friday, George handed me a carved wooden doll. It was five inches high, dressed in a white blouse, red vest, and embroidered black skirt. Her lips were painted bright red and her hair was dark and curly.

"Her hair's just like yours," George said. I uncoiled a curl as he spoke.

George spent hours talking to Arthur, Joanne's father. Arthur was a lawyer with a scraggly beard and a torn leather briefcase. He was always pulling some paper or other out of the case. Once, when they went to the store for cigarettes, I read a letter that they left on the dining room table. It was written on rippled onionskin paper, the kind that you use to send letters overseas. The letter was addressed to George Gonzales, 433 East 3rd Street, New York City.

"Dear Comrade, We need your help," the letter began. "We are organizing a rally of workers at Union Square on May Day and we need your support. A planning session is scheduled for March 15th in our Bowery headquarters. Please call BA 7-6538 to confirm that you will be attending. Sincerely, Robert Matthews, NYC Communist Party Chapter Secretary."

Communism was bad, I knew that. At the dinner table, my father often spoke about Russia and The Cold War. He was a fanatical defender of democracy, having experienced oppression first-hand when he was a boy in Poland.

"Be grateful," he said. "Be grateful that you are being brought up in this land of freedom. You can do anything. You can be anything you want. All you have to do is work hard."

I decided not to tell him about George and the letter. If I did, he would forbid me to hang out at Joanne's house.

On Saturday, when I arrived, Joanne was sitting on the living room floor, cutting strips of red and white paper. She was making daisy chains and she asked me to help her. They were for the rally next week.

"What rally?" I asked.

"It's a rally to make the government give poor people jobs and health care," Joanne said.

She didn't mention one word about the Communist Party.

"Here, I'll show you how to do it," she said, deftly looping a circle of red between her fingers, stapling it together and slipping a circle of white through the new loop. We sat on the linoleum, side by side, making daisy chains.

"Do you ever go to the rallies?" I asked Joanne.

"Sometimes," she said. "But not very often. The rallies are for grown-ups, not kids." She stopped speaking suddenly, a sign that she was not going to answer any more questions. We worked in silence, her chain growing twice as fast as mine.

George and Henry arrived half an hour later. They parked their gray Packard in front of the house and rang the bell. They were carrying four shopping bags, stuffed with papers. George dumped the papers on the table and began to sort the leaflets into piles.

"C'mon, girls, give a hand here," he said, pointing to the mess. "We need piles of 50." The leaflets were red and black. I picked up one of them and started to read:

"Workers of the World, Unite! You have nothing to lose but your chains."

There was a picture of two men, one white and one black, arms around each other. I could see the Flatiron Building behind them.

Arthur was on the telephone. His voice was loud and he seemed agitated.

"Be a little more careful," he said. "You don't want to get in trouble with the police, do you? You've been there before." He shook his head and whispered to George, "It's Paul. He was involved in a scuffle at City Hall this morning."

He glanced at me for a minute, wondering if he had been indiscreet.

I did not look away. My father always told me that turning your head made you appear guilty. "Don't put your head down when you've given the wrong answer," he said. "Keep your eyes open and your chin up." So, I flashed Arthur one of toothy smiles and he smiled back.

Arthur scrunched down in his chair and continued his phone conversation. "Try to avoid attention," he said. "Now's not the right time for confrontation." They made plans to meet on Monday morning. The last thing that I heard him say was, "Let's have breakfast in the Automat at 8:30."

After he hung up the phone, Arthur and George huddled. I had no idea who Paul was but I could tell that the run-in with the police was no minor matter. George wanted to come to the Monday meeting, but Arthur convinced him that it was better if he stayed away.

"There's no telling—they may be watching all of us," Arthur said softly. "I wouldn't be surprised."

During the following week, I scanned my father's newspapers, searching for news of the rally. On Wednesday, I found a four-paragraph story on the rally with a photo on page 16, opposite the obituaries.

The headline read: "Communist Party Rally at City Hall Draws Crowd of 500." I did not recognize anyone in the picture. The story under the photo gave an account of the rally, beginning with Richard Whyte's opening address on the rights of workers. Although the police were present just in case, there was no violence. The people in the photo were holding the leaflets that Joanne and I had counted.

"We are advocates for the working poor," Whyte told the crowd. "No one should go to sleep hungry."

I couldn't imagine going to sleep hungry. I thought for a minute of the glass of milk and plate of chocolate-chip cookies that was my bedtime ritual. The cookies were homemade—soft and chewy. When I ate them, the chocolate melted on my fingers and left a dark ring on my lips.

"There's plenty of work for people who want to work," my father said, over dinner, as he began the story of his passage to America, arriving here not knowing one word of English, OK. He had struggled and he had found work. If you didn't have a job, if you were poor and disadvantaged, it was your own fault. You were probably lazy or stupid. I had heard him give this speech a hundred times.

My father didn't think that race mattered. The only thing that mattered was your brain and your determination. I was thinking of Violet, the only black girl I knew. She hung out in front of the public library. Violet's dress was much too small and much too short and her shoes were too big. When the Good Humor truck stopped and the kids lined up to buy ice cream, she leaned against the wall of the brick building and watched. I wanted to buy her a toasted almond bar, my favorite, but I thought that she would be embarrassed by the offer.

Once in a while, Violet actually came inside the library. She sat in the reading room and turned the pages of the fashion magazines. We were only seats apart, but we never spoke. Violet's mother worked in the high school cafeteria. She stood behind the counter, with a white hairnet on her head, spooning dollops of mashed potatoes onto the heavy plates, then covering the mound of potatoes with ladlefuls of thick, brown gravy. I often saw her leaving the building, carrying a shopping bag of leftovers in each hand.

"No one has to remain poor," my father insisted. He was a man of one thousand stories, drawn from his life as a shoe salesman. "I once sold an old woman a pair of bright orange shoes," he said. "I convinced her that every time she wore them, they would cheer her up."

My father's economic optimism didn't convince me. "What if you lose your job or you're sick?" I asked him. I did not mention the newspaper story about the rally.

"Temporary setbacks," my father said, "minor obstacles on the road to progress." He took a deep breath, inflating his chest. No one could ever convince him that democracy had any flaws.

We sat in the living room playing chess. He was trying to teach me to be aggressive, to make bold moves and to take risks. My fingers rested on the knight for a moment but I lifted the pawn and moved it forward two spaces instead.

"Predictable," my father said. "You should have moved your bishop. There's nothing that you can do that will surprise me."

I laughed to myself. He had no idea what was going on in Joanne's house and I was not going to tell him. Suddenly, I felt emboldened. I looked down at the board and said, "Check."

My father reached over and tousled my hair. Then, without a word, he moved his castle and said: "Checkmate." The game was over.

It was hard to be bold in my working-class neighborhood. The main game was survival. The boys wore hand-me-down pants, and the girls dresses whose hems had been let down so often that their skirts sported a series of crease lines. Mothers filled out every meal with rice and potatoes. Everything was recycled. We were thrifty, too, but no one I knew went to sleep hungry and everyone seemed to have some sort of job. What distinguished us is that we were working-class folks with middle-class aspirations. They were just plain working class.

On my way to ballet classes, my mother would take a shortcut through the neighborhood by the train station. We traveled down Walnut Street for several blocks before heading east.

"Not a very good neighborhood," my mother said to me one day. "The houses are collapsing from neglect."

I looked out the car window, which was shut tight. Most of the people who lived on the blocks that intersected Walnut were black and Hispanic. They lived on welfare, my mother told me.

On the street corners, I saw gaunt men, gathering to talk and drink. They were worn and beaten.

"No jobs," my mother said, as we passed them by. "All they do is hang out."

Like my dad, my mother seemed to think they had brought their tragedy on themselves. If they would only behave, life would be good to them.

The men that I saw on the street had eyes that said otherwise. They were wounded creatures. I thought about the face of the black man on the leaflet for the rally. His eyes were clear. His back was straight. There was nothing wounded about him. He was fighting for his rights. He was marching for jobs. He was marching for these wounded souls on Walnut Street.

On Friday afternoon, my mother's throat was worse and she sent me to the drugstore for a bottle of red cough syrup, the kind that left a sickeningly sweet taste in your mouth. The store was two blocks away, at the intersection of Front and Main. As I turned the corner, a man, who was sitting in a black car parked at the curb hopped out and called to me: "Beverly Bluestein?" he said.

He was dressed in a dark blue suit. His skin was pale and he was wearing a straw hat. I had never seen him in the neighborhood before. He reached into his jacket pocket and pulled out a black case, which he opened with one hand. Inside was a badge that read "FBI."

Probably phony, I thought.

"You can check me out with Ed Ryan," the man said. "Just tell him that you spoke to Badge # 3596. Tell him that the code word is bait."

Ed Ryan was my high school civics teacher. He stood six-foot four, and he was at his best in the playground at recess when he joined the boys in taking shots at the basket. I liked him because he had an easy smile. But I knew better than to ask him too many questions.

The only bait that I knew was the killies that we hooked while still wiggling. Hooking a live fish made me sick. If you did it just right, they would continue to thrash—perfect bait for the larger fish in the dark waters.

"Tell him, the code word is bait," the man repeated.

I turned and entered the drugstore.

"Who was that man you were talking to?" Joey asked me. He kept an eye on us kids. If you lifted a candy bar, you could be sure that your parents would know about it the same day.

"He's a friend of my teacher, Mr. Ryan," I said, answering with a quick lie. "Last week he visited our class."

Joey seemed satisfied. He handed me the cough medicine and two pretzel rods, for free.

"Say hello to your parents," he said.

When I left the store, I was relieved to see that the black sedan was gone. A week earlier, I had heard a story that disturbed me. A girl named Carol came home after playing at a friend's house to find a note on the kitchen table. It was from her mother, who was a New York City schoolteacher. "We are down at the police station. Don't worry. Aunt Claire will be over at 6 PM."

Carol's parents were still in police custody. It was because they were Communists, my friend Joyce told me.

"It's very dangerous to even be near a Communist," Joyce said.

If that was true, I asked myself, what was I doing hanging out at Joanne's house every weekend? Unfortunately, I knew the answer to my own question. My home was safe, predictable, and law-abiding. Joanne's house was dangerous. It was filled with foreigners, strangers who spoke languages I did not understand. Papers were slipped into pockets. There were fierce political discussions around the dining room table, hushed private talks in the back bedroom, and whispered conversations on the telephone.

My father liked President Eisenhower. "Look at his face," he said to me, holding up the front page of The World Telegram & Sun. There was Ike, smiling. "You are looking at a leader, remember that," my father said. "Here is a man who understands how to fight a war and how to keep the peace."

Once, Dad gave me an "I Like Ike" button. "They were passing them out at the train station last year," he said, handing me the treasure which had been gathering dust in the top drawer of his bureau, next to three sets of cufflinks that he never wore.

The men at Joanne's house thought that Ike was a fool. He was dumb and predictable. America, they said, was getting what it deserved.

Ed Ryan agreed with my dad. He thought Ike was great, and he said so at our Friday session in the auditorium. After we pledged allegiance and saluted the flag, Ed walked up on the stage and spoke about America. We kids were fortunate. We lived in the greatest country in the world. We had the world's greatest leader, Dwight David Eisenhower.

Then he shut off the lights, pulled down the movie screen, and showed us footage of Eisenhower in Europe. There was General Eisenhower, addressing his troops, his short military jacket covered with medals.

Ed Ryan followed me to the lunchroom right after class. I was carrying my tray, with a plate of meatloaf with brown gravy, when he approached and asked if he could join me. He directed me to a table in the corner, far from the other kids, who sat at three long tables in the middle of the room. Ed wasn't eating. Instead, he was sipping from a large mug of coffee, tapping the fingers of his left hand on the table as he drank.

"You're friendly with Joanne Kahn, aren't you?" Mr. Ryan said. "You live right near each other, don't you?"

"Yes," I said. Mr. Ryan had me worried now.

"Are you there often?" he asked.

I wanted to lie. But I knew that he already knew the truth.

"I go there on the weekends," I said.

"There's a lot of activity going on there," Mr. Ryan said, "important stuff that would be very helpful to the FBI." He paused and waited

"Why would the FBI be interested in what's going on at Joanne's house?" I asked him. It was my debut as an actress.

"You tell me," he said. "You go there because you're attracted to the danger like a moth to a light."

As he spoke, I could see the moths swirling around my bedroom light fixture, one by one getting fried by the heat of the bulb. Sometimes, I could even hear the sound of their bodies sizzling.

"I hear that you met your contact," Mr. Ryan said. "It's your duty to help us. America is in danger. You can prevent a disaster."

His speech had become very dramatic and his eyes seemed larger. I was afraid. "I saw you once, carrying the flag in the Fourth of July parade on Main Street."

He was right. I had carried the flag, although I really didn't want to. I was given the honor because I scored the highest grade on the American History test. I was the only kid in the class who knew the first four paragraphs of The Declaration of Independence by heart.

I wanted to say "Stop. Don't speak to me any more." But I didn't. It was that moth-light attraction thing. For a moment, I imagined myself passing off folded notes to a man in a black car.

"We can work together," Mr. Ryan said. "All you have to do is report what is going on to me and I'll take care of the rest. Don't write anything down. We don't want anyone picking up your notes."

"I'll get in trouble with my parents," I said. That was an understatement. My father would lock me in my room if he ever found out. My mother would weep and pull her hair out and ask me what she had ever done to deserve such behavior. There would be no allowance for weeks. Maybe none forever.

"If they understood the importance of what you are doing, they would be proud of you," he said. "You're the only one who can help us because you can come and go in Joanne's house without arousing suspicion."

That was true. Nobody said a word when I showed up. Nobody asked me to leave when I sat there, reading comic books in the beat-up living room chair.

"What do you want me to do?" I asked. The thought of being a spy was appealing. I loved the sneaky characters in the movies, with their dark trench coats and foreign accents. The women smoked cigars and slipped sleeping pills into martinis. My life was utterly boring.

I was hoping that he would ask me to wear a tape recorder or carry a secret camera, just like the camera that I saw in the spy movie last week. It looked like it was small enough to fit in the pocket of my navy jacket.

"We believe that something big is being planned," Ed said. His face was grim and he stressed the word big. "We've tapped several phone calls. There is talk of a meeting within the next two weeks. We need you to find out the details. There's a public pay phone by the beach. We'd like you to call us whenever you can't reach me. Just dial 324-478-8700."

I knew that phone booth. The block was deserted. Two of the houses next to it had been boarded up for years. These guys were smart.

I imagined myself, in my homemade seersucker bathing suit, dialing the number. A man answered and said, "Hello."

"Killie," I said, giving my code name.

"Bait," he replied, waiting for my news.

"Two visitors from British Honduras arrived on Thursday. George and Henry dropped them off. They spent an hour in the back bedroom with Joanne's father. I saw him give one of them a blue passport. He told the other one to come back for his on Friday. One of the men crumpled a piece of paper and threw it in the wastebasket. When I was sure that he was gone, I rescued it. Printed in black letters was the name Ricardo Tovar."

"T-O-V-A-R?" my phone contact asked me.

"Yes," I said. "I'd heard that name before. Two weeks ago, I heard Arthur speaking to someone named Ricardo. Arthur suggested meeting him on a bench by the Ellis Island Ferry line but they decided to meet at Willie's, a coffee shop on 23rd Street and 8th Avenue."

"Did they ever meet?" the voice on the other end of the line asked.

"I don't know. I didn't hear the name Ricardo again until Thursday."

A woman appeared out of nowhere. She was dressed in flowered pink pedal pushers and her hair was up in pink plastic rollers. In her hand, she held a dime.

"Got to go now," I said. "Someone wants to use the phone."

There was a loud click and he hung up.

"Is it working?" the woman asked me as I opened the door to the booth. "Last week, I lost 30 cents here."

"It worked for me," I said. I scooted out of the booth and hurried up the block.

Ed touched my shoulder, bringing me back from my daydream. "You can do this," he said. "You're a clever girl and resourceful, too."

His hand was large and heavy. My shoulder drooped under its weight. There was no way that I could turn him down.

When I passed Joanne's house, the blinds were drawn. I could hear people arguing in the living room. The loudest voice was Arthur's. "Don't be a fool," he was saying. "Now's not the time to make a fuss."

"What do you mean fuss!" a man responded. He had a deep voice, with a thick foreign accent. It was not a voice I had ever heard before.

The phone rang and the voices went quiet. I was dying to know what was going on. But there was no way I could knock on the door now. Hanging around outside was risky too. The man sounded as if he was about to bolt out the front door.

Suddenly, there was a loud bang. It sounded like a gunshot to me, just like the booms that I heard in the Western movies, double features at the local theatre. I thought about going back to the phone booth and making a call. But I was not sure what I would say. I had nothing concrete to pass along.

My mother was in the kitchen when I arrived home. She waved at me, her right hand holding a potato masher. "How was school?" she asked, not stopping to look up.

This was our daily ritual.

"Got a 99 on my math homework and 'Excellent' on that book report," I said.

"As expected," my mother said. My mother was more forgiving than my father. When I missed four questions and received a 92 on an algebra test, he asked me, "What happened?" He looked over my paper, shaking his head, "These were much too easy to miss."

"Don't settle for second best," my father would say.

"Pay attention to details," my mother would always tell me.

I was not to disappoint them. They could count on me to be smart and reliable. There was no way that they ever could imagine me getting into trouble, in school or in life. They would never believe me if I told them that I was a spy, employed by the FBI to save America.

Thinking that thought made me shiver. Spying was a game to me. This was the first time that I thought of it as a job. We had never spoken about money and jobs were about money, weren't they? When I babysat for the family on the next block, they gave me two dollars for the evening, sometimes three dollars when they arrived home after midnight.

Now I was being asked to do something dangerous because I was patriotic. They were too smart to offer me money. What would I do with it? Buy things. That would make my parents suspicious.

After dinner, I walked past Joanne's house. The blinds were still closed. Their phone was ringing—but no one picked it up. For a moment, I thought I saw Joanne, peeking out of one window. There was a green Chevrolet parked in front of the house. It had Pennsylvania license plates. The tires were covered with mud. I had never seen it before. I continued walking to the corner, then turned around and began to walk back, on the opposite side of the street. I was two houses away when I noticed a woman in a brown suit leaving Joanne's. She stood on the stucco porch for a few moments, speaking to Arthur. He put his arm around her and gave her a hug. She was crying. "Call me the minute you get home," Arthur said. "Don't worry. I will take care of everything."

She walked down the stairs, car keys dangling in her hand. Within a few seconds, she revved the motor of the green Chevrolet and drove away. Arthur stood on the porch watching her leave. He looked upset. I thought about the loud noise. Had someone been shot and was there a body lying in their living room?

Joanne joined him on the porch. She caught sight of me and waved.

I wanted her to invite me up but she didn't. Instead, she walked down the stairs and joined me on the street. She was snapping her fingers—a sure sign that she was nervous.

"What's up?" I asked, counting the cracks in the sidewalk as we walked. "Nothing much," she said, barely looking at me.

"Can I sleep over your house tonight?" Joanne asked. "My parents are going out."

Usually, I slept over her house. Joanne preferred to sleep in her own bed. When the other girls had pajama parties, she always said no. Tonight seemed to be different. She didn't want to be home.

"I'll ask my mom and call you," I said, as we parted.

She crossed the street and ran up her front stairs, the porch door slamming behind her.

My mother was reading the newspaper when I got home. She had a pencil in hand, which meant that she was doing the crossword puzzle.

"The capital of New York State, six letters?" my mother asked.

"Albany," I said.

"A rock that is formed in layers, five letters?"

"Shale," I answered.

It was our little game. Most of the time she knew the correct answers.

"Joanne wants to sleep over tonight. Is that OK?" I asked.

"Sure," she said.

I called Joanne's number and she picked up on the first ring. "C'mon over," I said. In the background, I could hear people talking. Their voices were loud. "Don't do that," one of them kept saying.

"See you in an hour," Joanne said.

She showed up 45 minutes later, her red knapsack hanging from her shoulders. We sat side by side and finished our homework. Then, Joanne spied the Scrabble board and took it off my bedroom shelf.

We were not quite an even match. I won more often than she did, but she was scrappy and surprising. She loved to figure out ways to use up all of her letters. Once, she did so with the word testifies; another time she got a bonus of fifty points for the word indicted.

My strategy was different; I sought out the double and triple word and letters boxes, placing words ingeniously to cover them.

A half hour into our game, Joanne smelled victory.

"I've got you now," she said.

I no sooner placed the word code on the board, the c covering a blue triple score space, than she emptied the tiles from her rack, adding the seven letters to an s to spell subpoena.

"I know what the word means, too," she said, before I asked her. I've even seen a real one."

"What do you mean by real?" I asked.

"My father showed me," she said. "It's typed on crinkly white paper and has a light blue cover. If anyone rings the bell and tries to give me a folded paper with a blue cover, I am not supposed to take it."

"What does it say? I asked.

"It's an order," Joanne said, "An order from the court telling you that you have to appear and testify. Good people can get into serious trouble from subpoenas—my father told me so. They can ask you all sorts of questions and ruin your life."

"Not if they have your father as their lawyer," I said, hoping that my words would encourage her to tell me some bit of news that I could pass on.

"Sometimes, even my father can't help," she said, "and he can get in trouble, too. I say a prayer every night that he comes home safely."

"Who would kidnap him? I asked. Joanne had opened the door and I jumped right in.

"The FBI," she said. "They're dangerous. They pretend to be protecting us but they are really our enemy."

For a moment, Joanne's words made me feel like a traitor. Then, I recovered. She was brainwashed, I told myself. Her family and her father's friends— they were the enemies. I was on the side of the good guys.

"Why would the FBI be interested in your father?" I asked. "He helps poor people. Everyone loves him." I delivered the words with conviction, emphasizing everyone.

Joanne smiled. "You know that and I know that. But the FBI doesn't agree. They think that he helps spies and Communists and illegal immigrants." Her face flushed as she spoke. "They want those people out of America and they're mad at my father for helping them stay here."

"Eduardo?" I asked. "George? They're great guys."

"They're in big trouble," Joanne said. "Eduardo could get arrested any day now. My father begged him not to go to that rally but he did anyway. He's so stubborn. And more trouble is brewing next week."

She stopped speaking abruptly, aware that she was saying too much.

Our conversation was over. But she had definitely piqued my interest. I wanted to ask her about the loud noise that I had heard but I was afraid. It was now or never.

"I heard a loud noise when I was walking by your house," I said. "What happened?"

Joanne did not answer.

"Sounded like a gun shot to me," I said, not yet willing to give up.

Joanne began to chew the nail on her left pinkie finger.

"Well, it wasn't," she said. "And STOP asking questions."

The next morning, just before lunch, Ed Ryan stopped by my class.

"I need to speak to you," he said. "Meet me in my office after lunch."

We had not spoken for more than a week and I wondered if he was avoiding me. I ate my sandwich quickly, and then, jamming my apple into my pocket, walked up the three flights of stairs to Ed's office. The hallway was empty and I knocked on his door.

"C'mon in," a voice, unmistakably his, said.

Ed was sitting at his desk, reading.

"Lock the door, Beverly," he said, pointing to the latch.

"Read this," Ed said, handing me a folded piece of paper.

At the top of the paper, were the words: "Destroy this after reading."

Below, there was a message: "Speak to your contact at school. It's urgent. We need to know what she knows. Tell her to call us immediately."

"How do they know something BIG is up?" I asked.

"Simple," Ed explained. "They've got a tap on the telephone. They're listening in. But your friends are clever. They speak in code. We don't know what is about to happen or when. That's your job." I told Ed about the loud noise and about my conversation with Joanne.

"Call and get your instructions," Ed said. He stood up and handed me a book on the Indian tribes of New York State. "Here is the book you wanted to borrow," he said. "Return it when you have finished writing your report. You can share it with Joanne—her class has the same homework assignment."

I slipped the book into my knapsack and opened the door to leave. George Smith was standing outside, waiting to enter. George lived two blocks away from me. He was the tallest boy in our grade and probably the dumbest too.

"I need help," George said to me, as I left. "Hope he's in a good mood."

I raced down the stairs and headed to class. I'd make the phone call on the way home—but I couldn't imagine what they were going to ask me to do.

The bell rang at 3:00 PM and I headed for the pay phone. I dialed the number and waited for the man's voice. Killie, I said. A woman was on the line.

"Do you think that you can find a way to sleep over at Joanne's house tonight?" she asked me.

"I can try," I said, not exactly sure how I was going to pull it off. I hung up the phone and walked home. Joanne was sitting on her front steps, eating an apple. I sat down next to her. She offered me a bite.

"Do you think I can sleep over tonight?" I asked, without even saying hello. "My parents have to go out and I hate being alone. Maybe we could work on our Indian project together. Mr. Ryan gave me a great book."

Joanne ran up the stairs, calling her mother as she opened the front door.

"Can Beverly sleep over? We're working on a report and her parents are going out? Please. Please…."

She was inside the house for a couple of minutes. "My mom said yes," Joanne said, as she jumped down the steps, two at a time.

"I'll come back at 7:30 PM," I said, figuring that I would eat at home. "Mom says you should come over for supper," Joanne said. "We're eating at 7:00 PM. I think that we're having guests."

"See you later," I said, already preoccupied with trying to figure out what I was going to say to my mother.

I had told a lie. My parents weren't going out. Now, I had to tell another lie to make things work. The ironing board was set up in the corner of the dining room when I entered. On the floor, beneath my mother's feet, was a large wicker basket filled with my father's white dress shirts.

"I just baked cookies," Mom said. She did not look at me. She was concentrating on ironing the shirt collar—the hardest part.

"Joanne and I have a project due for civics," I said. "She's asked me to come for dinner and sleep over so that we can work on it together."

My mother lifted the iron and set it on its heel. There was a gush of steam.

"Tonight?" she said. She was studying my face, which usually gave me away. When I was nervous, my lips would often tremble.

"Yes, tonight. We really have to get it started. It will take days to get it finished."

She looked like she was about to ask me another question, but she didn't. Instead, she picked up the iron and returned to the collar.

"OK," she said. "But don't stay up too late."

I packed my knapsack and thought about the sleepover. Just before 7:00 pm, I got up to leave. My mother was reading one of her mysteries, curled into the corner of her favorite blue wingback chair. She looked up, over her reading glasses.

"I'll go straight to school in the morning," I said. "I took a change of clothing and my toothbrush."

"We're home all evening," my mother said. "Call if you need anything."

"You think I'm still a little girl," I laughed.

My mother roused herself from the chair, put her arms out, and gave me a big hug. I checked my knapsack to make sure that I had brought along the book that Mr. Ryan gave me. The entire junior class had the same assignment, a report on a New York State Indian tribe. I had already picked the Corchaugs, who had settled on the North Fork of Long Island, in the land near Peconic Bay. The beaches of Cutchogue and Southold and Jamesport were filled with Indian arrowheads and pottery shards. No one else would choose that tribe. They were too small, too unimportant.

By the time I arrived at Joanne's, the house was full. Arthur was home and Eduardo and George were there too. Paul arrived minutes after I did, carrying a large white box. Arthur said that they should wait until the others came before they opened it.

Joanne placed a plate of tuna fish sandwiches on the living room floor besides us. Then, we spread out our books. She had researched the Mohawks and thought that we should write our report on them. They were bold and powerful. I disagreed and took out Ed Ryan's book to show her the black and white photos of the Corchaugs who had inspired me.

"The Corchaugs were better. They made wampum, not war," I said. "We can build a three-dimensional diorama showing them making wampum."

Joanne was not convinced. I reached into my knapsack and pulled out a small brown bag. "Wait 'til you see these." I poured the contents of the bag on the brown shag carpet. There were clam and oyster shells with deep purple patterns, yellow and orange jingle shells, mother-of-pearl lined mussels, and pieces of twisted conch shells.

I took out a cloth sack, unknotting the green cord that was twisted around it. "I've brought some tools. We can make our own wampum."

Joanne fingered the shells. I had won her over.

"Hi, cutie," Eduardo said to her, as he sat down on the flowered chair near us. Eduardo was a chain smoker, a cloud of smoke swirled around his head.

"What are you two up to?" he asked. He reached over and picked up one of the clam shells. "We have these back home," he said. "I can show you how to carve them."

Eduardo took a small knife out of his pocket. "Very, very sharp," he explained, pointing to its odd blade. The doorbell rang. Arthur went to answer it and Eduardo closed his knife and stood up.

Two women and three men entered. I had never seen any of them before. They looked foreign, with dark hair, dark complexions, and dark clothes. Eduardo knew them. So did Arthur. I picked up a piece of clamshell, one with a deep purple color, and took out my file. I tried not to stare at them, concentrating instead on the shell. I handed Joanne a piece of coarse sandpaper and showed her how to smooth out the edges. We studied the pictures of wampum in our book. Most of the shells were shaped liked rectangles or triangles, varying according to their value and the tribe

Arthur joined us for a moment. "What are you girls up to?" he asked, fingering one of the purple shells.

"Wampum," Joanne answered.

"Funny money!" Arthur said. "Wouldn't we all be better off if we traded shells, instead of dollar bills?"

There were eight of them there now, too many for the back bedroom, which was small, most of the room taken up by the double bed and dresser.

They disappeared into the bedroom for a couple of minutes; then reappeared and sat down at the dining room table. They were going to hold their meeting ten feet from me. I was facing Joanne, who was facing them. Thank God they could not see my face.

"We're here to make sure that everything is in order for next week," Arthur said.

"Let's make sure that we're all on the right track," he continued. "Make it brief but give me all of the essentials. Who you've met with, and how things are coming along. Remember, code names only."

The first speaker had a strange accent, a strong v replacing her w. "I vant to tell you vat happened last Thursday," she said. "Ve vere supposed to meet at 62's house at noon. Vhen I valked up the block, I saw two men sitting in a parked car, near the corner. So, I kept on valking and didn't go in. I found a pay phone two blocks avay and called 62 vith the information. Ve changed our meeting place to 48's apartment, at 10 PM. They are on to something, that's for sure."

"Did you ever hold your meeting?" The voice was Arthur's.

"Ve did at 10," the woman said. "The street vas clear. Ve met in the basement. 62 read our instructions: 62 and 48 vere to exchange the briefcase in the vaiting room at Grand Central Station. They vere to sit in seats 17 and 18, vith their black leather briefcase on the floor in-between them. A voman in a green jacket vith an identical leather briefcase vould stop by. She vould place her briefcase down on the ground and talk to them for a few minutes; then leave vith their briefcase in hand. They vould remain seated for another fifteen minutes, leaving vith her briefcase."

Arthur interrupted her. "What was in the briefcase?" he said.

"Coded instructions for next week. Ve vill be following the Star Plan."

The clamshell broke in two. I had exerted too much pressure.

The phone rang and Arthur answered it. "Not much to report," he said to someone on the other end. "See you in town."

Arthur returned to the table and a man began to speak. He had a soft voice and I could barely understand what he was saying.

"They're on our trail, hot on our trail," he said. "Perhaps we should put off the action for a few weeks."

"Not possible," Arthur said. "We have our orders."

"Not if we're locked up in jail and that's what's going to happen."

The man stopped speaking for a few moments and someone sneezed.

"Agent 48, your report?" Arthur said. His voice now had a commanding tone.

"We're on target," Agent 48, a woman, responded. "We've met twice and our comrades are prepared. We have completely covered all aspects of airport security. We've done two run-throughs without a hitch. It took us exactly eight minutes to pick up the package and transfer it to the agent."

"Did anyone follow you?" Arthur asked.

"No one that we noticed," she answered. "But we were very careful. The package changed hands three times—always in a crowded place where it would be hard to detect the transaction. If you want to lose someone, do it at rush hour in Grand Central Station."

Agent 83 agreed. "Grand Central is good," he said, "but a subway platform is better. Exit the first car, hand the package to the next agent and leave."

"They're counting on us to pull it off," Arthur said. "Moscow is communicating with the Central Office on a daily basis. We are the infantrymen, the foot soldiers in the battle against capitalism."

Foot soldiers? Infantrymen? I didn't quite get what he was talking about but it was clear that he saw this as a massive struggle against the enemy, America. I was the only person who could stop them.

Joanne was busy with the wampum. She had already finished shaping and polishing the shells, drilling the holes and stringing two bracelets of orange and yellow jingles. "What do we do next?" she asked. We had yet to make our diorama.

"Do you have any cardboard?" I asked. She went into her bedroom and returned with a stack of cardboard. "I save them from my father's shirts. The Chinese laundry folds each shirt around a piece."

The cardboard was perfect, stiff enough to hold a shape but flexible enough for making teepees and longhouses. I drew a sketch of the village and asked Joanne to add her ideas. Joanne wanted one big central teepee, surrounded by four smaller ones, two on each side. The design I preferred was less symmetrical but I said that I liked hers better. It would make my job easier if Joanne was doing the building.

Arthur was on the phone again, checking a flight arrival at the airport. "Delta Flight 360," he asked, "from Dallas. On time. Great."

When he hung up, he asked Eduardo to go to the airport. "Agent 82 will be arriving on Flight 360," he said. "He will be wearing a green baseball cap with the letters ABC on it in yellow. Drive him to your apartment and wait for me to call you."

The meeting was breaking up. One of the women came over and bent down beside us. She fingered the wampum. Her long nails were painted a dark red. On one hand she wore an unusual gold serpent ring, two diamonds in the snake's eyes.

"Vhat is this?" she asked, in a voice with a heavy accent. She sounded like Zsa Zsa Gabor.

"Wampum," I answered. "Money made out of shells," I explained. "The natives in America, the Indians, used shell money like this."

I handed her a piece of wampum and looked up at her face. She looked like a movie star with her purple eye shadow and wine lipstick. Her eyebrows were arched and thin.

"Shells aren't worth much today," she said, laughing. "I don't think I could buy this with them," she said, patting her black alligator shoulder bag.

After they left, I wasn't sure how to proceed. I needed to get in touch with my contacts but could not make a phone call from the house. I would have to keep to the original plan, meeting them across from the drugstore tomorrow morning before going to school. They would be driving by the corner at 7:15 AM.

It was getting late. We decided to move the diorama, which was now half finished, to the corner of the living room, and go to bed. I went into the bathroom with a piece of loose leaf paper folded in my pocket. I had promised Ed Ryan not to take notes, but I had to. Inside the bathroom, I jotted down as much as I could remember—the agent numbers, the plans for the packages, the airport. I even described the woman, making sure to note that she had a large black mole on her right cheek. Then, I put the folded paper inside my right sock and decided to sleep with my socks on. There was a trundle bed in Joanne's tiny bedroom which, when pulled out, used up all of the available floor space.

Joanne climbed into her bed first. I pulled out the lower bed, shut the light, and climbed into mine. The bedroom door was slightly ajar and I could hear Joanne's father talking to someone in the hallway

"This has to go off like clockwork," he said. "We can't afford to make one little mistake. Here's $1,000 in twenties."

There was a muffled answer, followed by the slam of the front door, and silence.

A good spy would know what was going on by now. I was just an amateur, scribbling down notes.

I could not fall asleep. My eyes would not close and my brain would not turn off. I tried counting sheep but instead I found myself counting agents, each one stranger than the last one. They walked by hurriedly, disappearing into alleys, and sliding into the back seats of cars. I kept turning my pillow over and over again, seeking the comfort of the cool underside of the pillowcase.

Joanne was sound asleep, snoring lightly. Curled on her side, in a fetal position, she looked like a young girl of nine or ten. She was wearing bright red plaid flannel pajamas.

When I next looked at my watch it was nearly 7:00 in the morning. Joanne was still asleep and the house was quiet. My plan was to dress quickly and slip out of the house.

I was in luck. No one was in the living room. I took out a piece of paper and wrote a note: "Have to pick up my gym suit at home. See you later. Love, Beverly." Then, I opened the front door and tiptoed out. My timing was perfect. As I reached the corner, a black sedan pulled up. A man rolled down the window and said one word, bait. When I answered killie, the door opened and I slid into the back seat. The car made a right turn and we sped up.

I reached into my sock and pulled out my notes.

"I know that I wasn't supposed to take notes," I gushed, trying to head off any criticism, "but there were so many numbers that I was afraid that I would forget."

"No notes means no notes," the unknown man said, extending his tanned hand for the crumpled piece of paper.

"What was going on?" he asked. His question made me squirm. I felt like I was sitting in the first row at school, struggling to solve a difficult multiplication problem.

"There's an action planned for next week," I said. "It involves a package that is being passed from agent to agent and that is scheduled to leave the country on an airplane. They're worried that you will catch them." I paused to catch my breath. "I heard them say that the Central Office is speaking to Moscow on a daily basis. Eduardo was to meet Agent 82 who was arriving from Dallas on Delta flight 360 yesterday. He was to take him to his apartment."

The man took several pictures out of a manila envelope. "Do you recognize any of these people?" he asked.

The first photo that he showed me was one of the lady with the serpent ring. She was in a crowd and her faced was circled in black ink.

"She was there," I said. I did not recognize any of the other people in the photo that had obviously been taken at some public event and from a distance. Two men were holding a sign on which was printed the words: "Courage Comrades." Everyone was waving a little flag. There were some words written on them—but the letters were too small to read.

"What about this photo?" the man asked as he took out a second black and white image.

It was a photo of Arthur, Eduardo, and George in Grand Central Station. Arthur was shaking the hands of a tall man whom I did not know.

"You know who that is," I said. "You hired me to spy on him. That's Joanne's father," I said, pointing to Arthur. "And that's his two friends, Eduardo and George. George brought me a doll from a visit home to British Honduras. His last name is Gonzales and he lives in New York City. I once found a letter addressed to him in the living room wastebasket. He lives at 433 East 3rd Street. I don't know Eduardo's last name but he's in the house often."

"We know Arthur," the agent said. "Clever fellow—careful not to leave a trail. We have a bug on his office phone but he never makes a suspicious call from there. We follow him around but it's impossible to pin him down. Best we can do is a few pictures, like these. That's why we need you—to infiltrate his home."

I was surprised by his words. Arthur seemed sweet and innocent to me. He carried Lifesavers in his pants pocket and was always pulling off the green one, which he knew I didn't like, to uncover a red or yellow circle. It was impossible to imagine Arthur as a troublemaker, as an enemy of the United States.

"Arthur's no traitor," I said.

Joanne was my friend and Arthur was her father. He could end up in jail because of me. I hadn't thought about jail before.

I imagined Arthur in a prison cell. He was sitting on his cot, reading a letter from Joanne and he was crying. Joanne wrote about school and about me. "Beverly's my best friend, daddy, my most loyal, dearest friend. She's the only one who knows how much I miss you," Joanne wrote on the pink stationery that I had given her as a birthday present.

I was the traitor. Not Arthur. The rat-fink, turner-in, eavesdropping neighborhood spy! Rotten from head to toe. Disloyal. A liar. My nose would grow as long as Pinocchio's—that would be my punishment for betraying Joanne.

The FBI agent stared at me. "You're a real patriot," he said. "Think of what you are doing for your country."

I swallowed hard.

"What else can you tell me about the package?" he asked. "How big is it? Any clues about what might be in it?"

"It's small enough to fit in a briefcase," I said "and it contains something written in code." I remembered that Arthur had spoken about deciphering the information inside. "I heard them talking about a list of names and about detailed plans for future actions. Something was stolen from somewhere—I heard that too."

He frowned as I spoke. "Something and somewhere are not good spy words," he said. "You have to listen more carefully and be more specific."

My face flushed. "How am I to find things out if I don't hear them?" I asked belligerently. He had accused me of failing in my work. "I'm just a kid," I said. I had to fight off tears. I wasn't a crybaby, but the thought of failing as a spy was crushing.

As I spoke, I noticed that his scowl disappeared. He did not want to lose me. Something was better than nothing. I was inside the house while his men were outside.

I promised to pay greater attention.

"Call me every day," he said.

I shook his hand. It was cold and rough.

After school, I returned to Joanne's house. Joanne arranged six homemade chocolate chip cookies in a circle on a plate and went to the refrigerator for milk. There was none.

"I'm going to the store for milk," she said. "I need to stop at Catherine's for my science book. I'll be back in a half hour. Don't leave."

I nodded OK. I would be in the house alone. The thought of it made me shiver.

Joanne was out the door in seconds. I stood there shaking, then locked the front door. I walked into her parents' bedroom.

Across from the bed, there was a large desk—on it a stack of manila folders. I opened the top one. The first page had one word on it: SWAN. Below it, were the numbers 34, 56, 79, and 104. Someone had drawn a picture of a swan at the bottom in black ink. Letters of the alphabet marked its outline. A on the beak; B on its neck; C on one wing; D on one leg; E on another; F on its tail.

The next sheet was written in some sort of code. "On Tuesday at 11 AM, 34 will meet 56 at A; 56 will travel to C and wait for 79; 79 will wait three hours and travel to B. 79 will carry a large shopping bag. 79 will give the bag and contents to 104 at F, where 104 will wait for future instructions." The third page was a map of Queens, not far from LaGuardia Airport. The swan's outline was drawn over the streets. I noticed that its bill was on Ditmas Boulevard and its tail on 19th Avenue. There was a red X at the intersection of 46th Street.

I still had no idea what was happening. On the night table next to the bed, there was a worn black phone book. I leafed through it. The book had no names: only numbers. Number 34 had a Brooklyn phone number, easy to memorize: UL 3-4567. Number 56's number was a Barclay 7 exchange. I recognized it as Manhattan. BA 7-5432—even a five-year-old could remember that.

It was now fifteen minutes since Joanne left. I could not take the chance of getting caught. I went back into the living room, unlocked the front door and sat down on the couch. I tore a piece off of the newspaper next to me and wrote down the phone numbers that I had memorized. Then, I folded the paper into a tiny triangle and slipped it into my right sock.

I was thinking about swans. They were mean. "Never feed a swan," my father told me when we stood by the side of a small inlet to the bay. Three swans were swimming toward me. I was holding a handful of crumbled bread.

"They're beautiful, Daddy," I said. He took the bread from my hand.

"Beautiful but unpredictable," he said. It was the perfect occasion for him to deliver his "Don't be fooled by the outside of something" speech." I had heard it a million times. It usually started with "You can't tell a book by its cover." Within seconds, he would shift his lecture to girls who cared too much about their makeup or their dresses. He was afraid that I would become spoiled, like many of the girls who lived in the East End.

Joanne opened the door and slammed it behind her.

"Did you get what you needed?" I asked her.

She was carrying a brown paper bag in one hand, the science book in the other. She reached into the bag, took out the container of milk and handed me a Mounds bar.

"I brought you a present," she said, "for house sitting."

I laughed. Imagine, she was thanking me for spying on her family.

I broke the candy bar in half with my teeth and handed her the bigger piece. "No reason to thank me," I said. "In my house, you don't get a reward for hanging out and doing nothing!"

Joanne smiled. She had heard over and over again about my parents' work ethic. More was more. Less was never more. More was never less. I complained bitterly about the emphasis on grades and performance. She was lucky, I always told her. Her parents left her alone.

"We all get our own pressure," she said, rather mysteriously. "My parents may seem mellow to you but they have their own agenda. They insist that I agree with their opinions."

"Like what?" I asked, jumping at the opening.

"Workers' rights," Joanne said, "and capitalism. Capitalism's corrupt. Rich people are getting richer and poor people poorer. The working man is the victim. And the U.S. government is to blame, that's what my parents think."

"And do you agree?" I asked.

"They're probably right—but, sometimes, I am not so sure. I've talked to people who lived in Russia under the Communists and they sound afraid— afraid to speak their mind, afraid to meet with their friends, afraid to be seen in the wrong place." She paused and then added, "It's not much better here. My parents tell me that the FBI follows everyone around. They're clever, you know. They turn everyone into spies."

Her face was blank and it was clear that she was not fishing for information. Still, it scared me. I would never be able to handle her interrogation.

Joanne was in the mood to talk. The candy bar had clearly loosened her tongue.

"I know a few spies," she said, "and you do, too!"

I waited.

"Eduardo, he's a spy," she said, glowing as she spoke. She knew that she was breaking the rule and telling me something that she shouldn't.

"I trust you," she said, "That's why I'm telling you. Eduardo is a spy. He does very dangerous work."

"Who does he spy for and what does he spy about?" I asked.

"For the Communists," Joanne said. "He's always on the phone with someone named Boris. I found Boris's phone number on a slip of paper once, BA 7-5432."

That was the number in my sock. So, Boris was Agent 56.

"Eduardo carries a gun," Joanne said. "I've seen it bulging under his jacket."

Joanne stood up and put on the television set. Her body language told me that she had absorbed the sugar from the candy bar and that our talk was over. We sat side by side watching The Lone Ranger. He had a gun. But he was a hero, not a spy, an American hero. We loved the way he tipped his cowboy hat. We loved the way his horse kicked up dust as he and Tonto rode off after the bad guys.

The bad guys had bloodshot eyes and heavy beards. They drank too much. They played cards. They flirted with women in the local saloon. The good guys had clear eyes and they were clean shaven. They could hold their liquor and win a hand at poker. They treated their women right.

Spies were another story. Eduardo was a spy. I was a spy.

Not a very experienced one, though. I was feeling torn. If I managed to get inside information, I could ruin Joanne's family and send her father to jail. They might even lock up my best friend. But my country was in danger. The Communists were everywhere and Russia might just win the Cold War. That would be the end of all of us. We'd lose our homes. We'd lose our freedom.

After I left Joanne's, I walked up the block to the beach. The surf was rough and the tide was going out. I took off my shoes and walked in the wet sand. I had to call my contact, but I was afraid. I could hear my father yelling at me: "How did you ever get into this mess?" I could hear my mother wailing: "What did I tell you Beverly? Look behind you." I could see Arthur shaking his finger at me: "You sat in our house and you betrayed us!" Joanne just stared at me in disbelief. She had no words for me. No tears either—just rage, anger, shock, and pain. I closed my eyes and Joanne faded from view. She would have to understand. They all would.

I brushed the sand off my toes and put on my socks and shoes and walked to the pay phone, clutching the scrap of paper with the numbers. Within seconds, I was through to my contact.

"They're in action," I said, reading off my list of numbers and describing the swan drawing in great detail. "It's set for Tuesday." He interrogated me for several minutes, making sure that he understood everything that I had overheard. Then, without a thank you, he said, "Get back to us, if anything new develops." There was a loud click as he hung up the phone.

We still had not finished the diorama—so we decided to meet late the next afternoon to finish the project. When I arrived, Joanne was agitated. She was shredding a napkin in her fingers.

"You finish it," she said as I sat down beside the cardboard village. "I can't deal with cutting and pasting today." Her fingers were trembling, something I had never seen before.

I could hear her mother talking on the kitchen phone.

"Will you be coming home tonight?" she asked, whispering, "I hope so. I'm afraid." She hung up the phone and continued washing dishes. Within seconds, I heard a glass shatter as it hit the tile floor.

"Don't know what's wrong with me today," she muttered.

The phone rang a second time. Joanne's mother picked it up quickly.

"Call him at Eduardo's," she said. "He'll be there for two hours. After that, they'll be at Ana's apartment on Tremont Avenue."

Ana was the woman with the red nails and the thin eyebrows.

I was surprised that Joanne's mom was speaking so openly on the phone. Arthur was much more careful. Ten minutes after I arrived, Joanne's mother left.

"I'll call you later," she said, rather mysteriously, to Joanne who began to cry the minute after her mother closed the door.

"I'm going to end up an orphan," she said, shaking her head from side to side. "I'll be an orphan with two live parents who are locked up in jail!" Joanne wailed.

"Who would want to lock up your parents?" I asked.

Joanne hesitated before speaking. Then, desperate to share her news, she explained.

"A friend of my father's has been arrested for anti-American activities. He's not a citizen and they are holding him in a detention center somewhere in New York City."

"Have I met him?" I asked, trying my best to encourage her to keep talking.

"I don't think so," she said. "It's Manuel, a friend of Eduardo's. Manuel's been here but only late at night. He runs errands for my father."

"What sort of errands?" I asked.

"He delivers packages and messages—in code, of course. But he got caught with a message yesterday and everyone's scared that the cops know about the big operation."

"The big operation?"

"It's happening on Wednesday. We're sending a list of U.S. spies to Moscow. It took almost two years to find out who these people are. We've got their code names too." Joanne stopped to catch her breath. "I'm not supposed to know all of this but I do."

When Joanne used the word we, it rattled me. That made her my enemy too.

"It'll blow the cover on the whole American spy operation," she said.

"Dad says that all of the plans have to change now. Instead of passing the names along on Wednesday, we are going to switch it to Friday at 5:00 PM—rush hour on the downtown 34th Street C train platform. Eduardo was supposed to be in charge. But Manual might squeal on Eduardo, so Ana will be taking over." She reached for a tissue and blew her nose.

There was no point trying to console her. In fact, I wasn't sure that I could do a convincing job. She had just given me the inside dirt on the operation. I was her best friend, the only one she could trust. Here in the West End, where only a few of us didn't decorate the front windows with Christmas lights and shamrocks on St. Paddy's Day, life could be lonely. Outsiders like Joanne and me bonded. How could I betray that friendship?

"You might have to visit me in jail," Joanne said. "They could arrest me too."

"They don't arrest kids," I said. I was at a loss to say more. Part of me wanted to comfort her. The other part wanted to get out of there as fast as I could to pass along my new information.

When I was ten, I ratted on my friend Flora. She told me that her parents were fighting and that they were getting divorced. I told every other girl in the class. Flora was furious and she dumped me.

"How could you do this?" she asked. "I trusted you. You were the only person I told." She spit in my face. When I came home, I locked myself in my room and would not come out for dinner.

"What's wrong?" my mother asked, speaking to me through the keyhole.

"Nothing. Everything," I said. After a couple of hours, I let her in.

"Let that be a lesson to you," my mother said. "Friendship is precious. When you betray a friend, you betray yourself."

I knew that Joanne would be even angrier than Flora. I wasn't sure what she would do but she had a temper. I had a temper, too. Maybe that was why we were such good friends. I picked up a piece of cardboard and began to cut out a teepee, by drawing a semi-circle and then rolling it into a cone shape. Using colored pencils, I decorated the shape with Corchaug motifs. Joanne made no effort to help me. She sat, hunched over, holding her head up with one hand. I made a second teepee, anchoring the teepees to the base of the diorama.

"Looks great, doesn't it?" I said.

Joanne did not raise her eyes.

"You're a real buddy," she said, barely moving. "There's no one in the whole world I would trust more than you."

There was the sound of a key in the front door. Joanne ran to the bathroom to wash her face. Her mother entered. She was carrying two shopping bags. "Where's Joanne?" she asked. Her face was drawn and there were dark circles under her eyes. Always thin, she looked emaciated now.

"In the bathroom," I answered.

She hung her coat in the front closet and carried the two bags into her bedroom. I heard her dialing a phone number.

"Got the stuff," she said. "There was no problem. Are you OK?"

She was talking to Arthur. I could tell that by the way she said OK. It was the way my mother spoke to my father.

Joanne was out of the bathroom now.

"Something wrong?" her mother asked, scrutinizing Joanne's face.

"I got an eyelash caught under my eyelid," Joanne said. "It was stinging and stinging. But I think I got it out."

She moved closer to her mother to let her examine the eye.

"It's all red from rubbing it," her mother said. "But there's nothing there." She kissed her on the forehead and walked into the kitchen.

"Better get home," I said, reaching for my jacket which was lying on the couch. "There's not much left to do," I said. "Let me take it home and finish it." We packed up all of the cardboard and the shells and the colored pencils and put it in large brown shopping bag.

Outside, I walked toward my house. But I didn't go in. Instead, I walked around the block and headed for the pay phone by the beach.

"Are you sure," a voice asked me after I relayed the plans. "Are you 100 percent sure that this is going down this way?"

"One million percent!" I answered. "I heard what I heard."

"We can't afford to make a mistake," he said.

"You're not going to lock up my friend Joanne," I said.

"Of course not," he answered.

By the time I got off the phone, my palms were sweaty. I couldn't take it back now. Being a spy was glamorous but it was treacherous too. My mother was making macaroni and cheese for supper. I could smell it as I climbed the stairs to the front porch.

"Set the table," my mother said, as I dropped my knapsack and the shopping bag on a dining room chair.

"How are you?"

"The diorama's almost done," I said. "I brought it home to finish it."

"Do you like it?" my mother asked.

"Yes," I said.

"Does Joanne?"

"I suppose so."

I set the table, so lost in thought that I placed all of the forks on the right side of the plates.

"What's on your mind?" my mother asked as she moved the forks.

"Nothing," I said.

My father arrived. He dropped a pile of newspapers on the couch and sat down at the dining table. " I'm starved," he said to my mother.

We sat down to eat, our plates piled high with steaming macaroni and green beans. My dad poured himself a beer.

"There was a police action in Union Square today," my father said. "They arrested two men who were handing out Communist Party fliers. The men resisted and the police hit them on the head with their clubs."

"The police were just doing their job," he said. "They're just troublemakers. I never take their fliers," he said.

All of a sudden, I wasn't hungry. I dipped a green bean into the cheese sauce and nibbled on one end. The mound of macaroni overwhelmed me. I stabbed my fork into the middle.

"Stop playing with your food," my mother said as she watched me attacking the pasta.

I pulled my fork out of the macaroni. Both of my parents were staring at me.

"Why don't you take their fliers?" I asked my dad.

"You're too young to understand," he said, scraping up the last of the cheese sauce from his plate with his finger. "The Cold War isn't just talk."

I forced myself to eat a little, then asked to be excused. There was nothing to do but wait now, wait and worry. I lay down on my bed and tried to fall asleep. I could hear my parents talking. My father was still ranting about the Commies and the Cold War. I pulled the covers over my head to muffle the sound.

The next day I didn't see Joanne in school. We usually met in the lunch room but she wasn't there. In the afternoon, when I walked by her house the blinds were drawn. I knocked on the door but no one answered. Later that evening, I called her home, but gave up after eight rings.

No one was there Thursday, Friday, Saturday, or Sunday, either.

I was worried. The operation was to have taken place on Friday. No one had contacted me. I scanned the newspapers but there was no news. Frantic, I walked to the pay phone and called my contact.

"Where's Joanne?" I asked the voice at the other end of the line.

"You did good work," he answered.

"Where's Joanne?" I asked again.

"It's not your problem. Your job is done."

I hung up the phone and walked home. My knees were shaking and my balance was unsteady. I felt nauseous. When I reached the corner, I leaned upon the lamppost and threw up. I kept heaving and heaving, until I was empty.

Monday was a quiet day. There was not a sign of life at Joanne's house. In the evening, there were no lights.

On Thursday, when I came home from school, I checked the mail. There was a post card for me, with a picture of the Empire State Building on it. The handwriting was Joanne's. "Beverly, I didn't want to leave without saying good-bye," she wrote. "You will always be my best friend. Love and Kisses, Joanne." Her signature was blurred. It looked like she had been crying. The card was postmarked Chicago.

I placed the card inside my red leather diary, zippered it all around, and locked the key. I was the reason for all of her troubles. I had betrayed her. What a rotten friend I was.

That spring, I felt very lonely. My grades fell. My parents tried to talk to me.

"What's wrong?" they asked.

I could never tell them. I could never tell anyone. I carried my betrayal around like a lead weight, banging against my barely developed chest. Thump, thump. Bang. Bang. Bruising my skin. Bruising my soul. Beverly the spy. Beverly the betrayer.

Watching for the Enemy

1 9 5 7

IT STOOD, PERHAPS, 150 FEET FROM THE BEACH, 200 feet from the Atlantic Ocean at high tide—a concrete monolith against the grey sky. Three stories tall with slits for windows near the top, it was an odd building that did not resemble the typical two-story wooden structures along the boardwalk.

The local kids said that ghosts lived there. They had seen them slipping out of the slits at dusk to circle in the night air. A family of ghosts holding hands by their pinkie fingers as they flew over the deserted white sand.

Jimmy heard them singing one evening, a song about digging to China, digging down through the wet sand, to the other side of the world where people ate with chopsticks and slept on straw mats.

I knew they were wrong. I had actually been inside. Not with permission, mind you but once, on my way home from closing the amusement park, I walked by the tower and noticed that the back door was ajar. The wind was ferocious that day and one of the hinges on the door lay broken on the ground, near large splinters of wood.

The old men on the boardwalk had a million stories about the tower, which was last used in 1945. Ten years later, they remembered the commander stationed there, a man in his fifties, his Coast Guard uniform neatly pressed and his black shoes shiny. He arrived like clockwork at 8:00 AM to inspect the station, speak to the men who were signing out from their nighttime duty, and read the reports.

Manny, the owner of the cotton-candy booth, told me that a dozen enemy subs were seen from the tower during the Second World War. In 1943 alone, six subs were spotted lurking off the beach.

I thought about Manny's words when I walked past the tower. It had been abandoned since the end of the war, and the kids at the amusement park were always aiming their slingshots at the top windows. I shooed them away, stopping occasionally to read the small brass plaque that was bolted to the wall.

"Dedicated to the men whose sharp eyes valiantly protected our country from the forces of evil. Mayor Ralph J. Serrano. June 30, 1947."

I had never met those valiant men but I did know Sandra and Stuart, a couple of boardwalk regulars. On a sunny summer afternoon, Sandra, hidden by her straw sunhat and her yellow sunglasses, occupied the bench directly opposite the skeeball parlor. No one else dared sit there. There she was, in all her glory, perched on a striped beach towel, waving at the children who skipped by.

Sandra dispensed candies from a purple sack and knew all of the children by name. They hovered around her like beach flies around an abandoned watermelon rind, waiting for the candy, waiting for a sweet story.

Sandra fancied herself the boardwalk historian, even though she was only 23 years old. She had lived near the boardwalk since birth and had spent her whole life walking the wooden planks. She carried a red spiral notebook, jotting down in pencil descriptions of everything and everyone she met.

Stuart was Sandra's boyfriend. He sold hotdogs and soda in the last booth by the poker arcade and he'd been coming to the boardwalk since he was 11 years old. Stuart sported a perpetual tan and a cigarette and he wore bold checked shirts. You couldn't miss him—nor Sandra for that matter, since they spent most of their spare time together, holding court on adjacent benches.

Sandra was a switchboard operator at The Columbus. She worked the graveyard shift, from 6:00 to midnight five days a week. When she wasn't connecting the gray trunk lines in the hot back office, she could be found on her bench, spinning yarns.

Working the switchboard meant that Sandra knew everyone's business. She knew all of the mistresses and when to connect them to the rooms. She knew all of the wives and the children, too. At the end of the summer, Sandra got big tips for her discretion from husbands who had cheated and wives who had had a summer fling with a busboy or a waiter.

Sandra and Stuart had been together for nearly a year now. They were Mr. and Mrs. Boardwalk—a walking, talking archive—always ready to recount their memories, real or imagined, of the good old days when the women strutted up and down in their striped peddle pushers, shimmering sling-back sandals trimmed with rhinestones on their feet, and the men paraded back and forth, decked out in chartreuse shirts, trimmed with white fringe, and pleated white linen pants.

It was Sandra who claimed to know the real story about the lookout station where the men kept their binoculars pointed at the sea, watching for enemy subs.

"I snuck in there last year when the wind blew the door open," I confessed to Sandra one day, when I was sitting by her side having my lunch. "Didn't find much. A few old notebooks, a metal desk with a green linoleum top, six or seven high wooden stools, and an Emerson radio. What a view of the ocean. When you look out through those slits of glass, you can see miles out."

Sandra tore open a bag of potato chips with her teeth and offered them to me. "That was an important lookout," she said, crunching loudly as she spoke. "The Germans and the Japs had to be very careful when they were close to shore. One false move and it was over. One mistake and we could blow them to pieces."

Sandra did not need coaxing to tell the rest of her story. "I saw a sub once," she said. "I was visiting the guys in the tower when one of them caught sight of a sub and started screaming. He was jumping up and down and they all took turns looking through the lens to be sure he was right. I begged for a peek and they let me look—just for a second."

I didn't believe Sandra. There was no way those guys would have let a nine-year-old kid look at an enemy sub. But she sure knew how to tell a story. After hours at the rides, where I spent my day strapping kids into go-carts and toddlers onto carousel horses, the stories were just what I needed.

"It had three swastikas on the top," Sandra continued, "and you knew it was a Nazi sub the minute you looked at it. I was scared, really scared, that they were going to land and capture all of us." Sandra took a deep breath, reached into her pocketbook, pulled out a mirror and a tweezers, and, without saying a word, plucked a hair from between her eyebrows. "Really scary," she continued, "my knees were knocking—bang, bang, bang, like a drum." Sandra banged her hand on the bench, making a loud knocking sound.

"Those guys were Nazis and they were close, too close for me. They were going to drop someone off, at least that's what the guys in the tower said. So they pressed the red alert button and a light lit up and someone sent a secret message telling the Coast Guard that the enemy was near and…"

"I don't believe you," I said, interrupting Sandra. "Never heard that one before." But I had heard little about the tower and was not a local, having come to the boardwalk to run the amusement park after a childhood spent hanging out in front of a candy store in the Bronx. I had heard that there were sightings of subs, but no one who was sane believed the rumors of spies dropped off in the middle of night.

"You weren't there, Arnold," Sandra said. "So, you can say what you want to but you're wrong, just plain wrong. I was there and I tell you it was a German sub and the reason it was so close to shore was that they wanted to drop off a spy—which they didn't do that night but they did do one week later. I was told that for a fact by one of the officers."

Sandra reached into her beach bag and took out a tangerine. Slowly, she began to peel it, carefully arranging the peel so that it would not fall through the bench slats. I could see that she had already dismissed my comments and that she was going to tell the whole story of the German spy who came ashore, whether I believed it or not.

"One week later, the sub came close again, only this time, no one spotted it from the tower. They landed two spies on the beach—at least that's what the Coast Guard officers figured out later from the footprints of their regulation Nazi boots, that were still there the next morning, clearly marked in the sand under the boardwalk, next to a cigarette butt that was definitely German.

"Where they went, nobody ever found out. They vanished into thin air despite a thorough investigation. The officers knocked on the apartment doors of everyone who lived in the apartment buildings and hotels along the board-walk, asking the same questions: Did you see anyone last night? Did you hear anything strange? But no one had seen or heard a thing.

"Years later, the rumor was still circulating that one of the spies had settled nearby, having abandoned his allegiance to Germany once the Nazis were de-feated. There was a fellow with a thick German accent who lived in the Rose-dale Arms, two blocks from the tower.

He earned a few dollars by sweeping the sand off the sidewalk in front of the hotel and shoveling snow and chipping ice in the winter. His name was Hermann and he kept to himself. But along the boardwalk there was talk that Hermann was one of the spies who had landed there during the war.

"Before he disappeared, I talked with him often," Sandra told me. "He'd been to Berlin and to Frankfurt and Paris and London. We never spoke about spying though he wore a strange little gold ring that I'm sure used to hold secret code."

I laughed when Sandra said that. "What a vivid imagination you have," I said. "You've been reading too many ads in the back of comic books." I was thinking of all of those cheap metal spy rings that you could buy for a quarter. The kids on the rides always wore them, showing off their latest trophy to one another as they rode by on different colored horses.

"Hermann was definitely a spy," Sandra continued. "You didn't need to be Sherlock Holmes to figure that out. He always looked behind him when he walked and he had an odd habit of tearing up little notes into tiny pieces. He never spoke about family either."

"He was very proud of his collection of postcards and he showed them to me often. Hermann was a regular encyclopedia—he knew exactly how tall the Eiffel Tower was, he could tell you how many windows there were in the Reichstag. He kept his cards arranged carefully in groups, separated by rubber bands in a Florsheim Shoe box, carrying it out weekly for his show n' tell."

"Did you ever get your courage up to ask Hermann about the spies?" I asked. "I mean it would have been real easy to catch him in a lie." She had me hooked.

"That's what you think. He was much too shrewd to be caught. One Friday, he didn't appear on the boardwalk. I went to his apartment but no one seemed to have seen him. Two weeks later, a new man was sweeping the sand off the sidewalk in front of his building. Hermann had vanished."

She took off her shoe and turned it upside down. A stream of fine, white sand trickled on the wood, leaving what looked like a letter H on the wood. "There," Sandra said, "Hermann has heard me and he's sent me a sign."

I laughed at her craziness. "Doesn't look like an H to me," I said. I wasn't impressed with Sandra's divining. She wasn't a convincing gypsy and I was sure that she couldn't find the lifeline on my palm if she tried. I stared at my hand as I listened to her. My lifeline was broken halfway across—a sharp, definite break. I curled my fingers into a tight fist to conceal it and stared back at her.

"It's an H, all right," she said. She kicked the sand with her left foot, scattering it in several directions. "Hermann told me that he'd been inside the tower and I believed him. He could describe it precisely—the concrete walls, the maps pinned to a bulletin board that were marked with little red dots. Those dots were like the markings in the police station, the exact locations of the crimes. Only in this case it was where the subs had been sighted. Hermann knew the history of every one of them."

What an irony. Here was this guy who Sandra was sure was a German spy, a man who had crept ashore in the middle of the night, now functioning as the neighborhood expert on sub sightings. Hermann could explain all of the markings, the little red stars and circles. Of course, he knew. After all, who had trained him? The German Navy. "Could he have been a double agent?" I asked. "Working with both sides?"

Sandra shook her head, no. "Hermann was no double agent. He was a German spy who found a way to live here, by the boardwalk, without getting intro trouble—at first. But something happened, I'm sure of it. Someone caught on to him. Why would he have just disappeared one day?"

Sandra asked the local police about Hermann. But all they would tell her was that there was an ongoing investigation. "I spoke to my buddy Sergeant O'Brien who walked the boardwalk. O'Brien was a regular and, if anyone knew the truth, it was he. But he had nothing to tell me. He just threw his hands up in the air. I could tell from the look in his eyes that there was more to the story."

Sandra interrupted her storytelling to greet Stuart, who had just gotten off from work. He planted a big kiss on her red lips. "How's my baby?" he said. Then, laughing, he added, "Still talking!"

"I'm telling Arnold about Hermann," Sandra said. Stuart took a can of coke and a sandwich out of a blue knapsack and sat down. "Are you hungry, honey?" he asked.

She shook her head no and resumed her story. "O'Brien knew something all right. But he wasn't going to tell me. During the next couple of weeks, I passed the Rosedale daily, hoping to catch a glimpse of Hermann, but he was not to be found. I gave up looking for him. I had better things to do with my life." She laughed at her own words, finding something funny in her admission.

It was hard for me to imagine what those better things were or why they were so funny. She seemed more concerned with the chips on her red nail polish than the state of the world.

"Did you ever hear of Senator Joseph McCarthy?" she asked me, pausing in her tale of Hermann. "Thank God, he died," she said. "He was a real spy." She tugged at a long strip of red nail polish, and peeled it off triumphantly. "He was evil, looking for Commies everywhere. I saw him on television once."

I wasn't entirely sure how or why Sandra had shifted from Hermann to

McCarthy–except that in a strange way it made sense to me. Enemies were everywhere. You couldn't be too careful.

"Did you think Hermann was spying on us?" I asked Sandra, in an effort to bring her back to the story.

"Of course," she said. "That's why I loved talking to him. Everything he said had a hidden meaning. At least to me, it did. He could rattle off statistics so fast—the length of the sub, its speed above and below water, the number of torpedoes it carried. He was completely obsessed with unterseebootwaffe."

She didn't have to translate the word for me. I knew that she was talking about German U-boats, the ones that beached by the tower during the war. One of which, Sandra was sure, had dropped Hermann off on the beach by the boardwalk.

"Those U-boats were like alligators, swimming through the Atlantic, their eyes above water," Sandra continued. "Their grey hulks slipped silently through the waves while the men in the tower watched and waited, charting their movements on three-square-foot sheets of pale green graph paper thumb-tacked to the walls.

"You couldn't be too careful. The newspapers reported on the battles in Europe, but we knew that there was trouble here, too." Sandra's voice took on an authoritative tone, the register of a lecturer at the podium.

"Weren't you aware of the spies?" she asked me incredulously. I could hear the disbelief in her voice and feel the sting of her criticism. "Every kid with a German-sounding last name was suspect," she continued. "There was a girl with thick eyeglasses. Greta, I think that was her name. Greta Schultz. She wore a plaid jumper and her hair was always in neat braids. She carried her lunch in a strange, little metal lunch box which her mother had brought to America from Munich. Greta's mom, Bertha, had come here as a young woman and met and married her father, Heinz, who had also emigrated to the U.S. from Hamburg. That lunch box was a dead give-away. They were Nazis—and that meant that Greta was not welcome in our girls' club."

"You girls were just as evil to her as McCarthy was to the people he called Communists. Once you scout for enemies, you find them everywhere," I said, emphasizing the word everywhere.

"Not everywhere," Sandra insisted. "Just almost everywhere." She stared at me and did not blink, as if to say, you may think you're smart, but you're definitely not as smart as I am, so don't take me on. Don't be a wise guy, Sandra's eyes said, or else. I knew that it wasn't good to mess with the Sandras of this world. They just might punch you in the nose or at the very least throw a glass of soda in your face.

"Hermann didn't have a wife or any children that I knew of," Sandra continued. "But if he did have a daughter, she would have looked like Greta. Blonde and ruddy-cheeked. Big-boned and solid. All of those Germans were the master race, you know."

I could tell that Sandra hated Greta and that she also was obsessed with Hermann, the spy who sat on the bench next to her, spinning yarns.

"After Hermann disappeared, the tower was locked up for years," Sandra said. "The war was over and the lookout was no longer needed. Every year, on Halloween, the neighborhood kids met outside the tower to tell ghost stories. It was the spookiest place in town, pitch black—except for the shimmering circles made by their flashlights. One Halloween, Billy, who was 15 and nearly six feet tall, got the idea to smash the lock and let the kids in. He found a big rock and pounded on the padlock which, after years of sea air, was badly rusted. It broke by the time the kids counted to 107. The little kids were too scared to go in. But Billy, followed by the teenagers, pulled open the door and walked slowly up the concrete stairs."

She had me now. I felt my hands tremble and I was swallowing hard. I was scared of that tower, too. Even I, who had been inside, feared the worst.

"Those kids shouldn't have done that," I said. I was prodding Sandra to continue the story. I'm not exactly sure why I said it, since I knew that had I been there I definitely would have been one of the leaders. "What happened?" I asked, anxious to get Sandra to continue the story.

"Billy reached the top of the stairs first and he shone his flashlight on the floor. All of a sudden, he began to scream. The kids didn't know why he was screaming but they began to scream, too. And they also began to run down the stairs in a mad stampede. Billy and his best friend, John, stayed behind, while the rest of the kids huddled outside, waiting for their return.

"Billy was pretty shaken. He'd seen a skeleton in the tower. A real skeleton. A skeleton on, of all days, Halloween. Within seconds, the band of trick-or-treaters headed north in the direction of the police station that was located about a mile away. They marched silently, stopping several times to look behind them.

"The sergeant in the police station laughed when he heard their story. He was certain that it was a Halloween prank. He'd investigate it but not 'til the next day. Not good enough, the kids insisted. They were not playing a prank. There was a skeleton in the tower, no fooling.

"The next morning, a police car drove up to the tower. Two cops checked the broken padlock and climbed the stairs. One of them radioed in a call to the station, 'The kids were telling the truth,' he said. 'There's a skeleton here, all right.'"

Sandra stopped to take a sip of water. "They never did find out who it was," she said. "Dental records showed nothing. But I know who he was," Sandra said. "I know for sure who he was. It was Hermann. Don't know how he got there. But I'm certain it was Hermann. Hermann, the spy, buried in his concrete tower tomb."

Sandra stood up and looped her arm through Stuart's. "You probably don't believe me," she said.

Actually, I did.

Skeeball

July 1958

IT'S NICKELS THAT I NEED. Two hundred rolled packs of nickels can pretty much take me through the morning on a slow day. I have my own system. Two whacks against the metal drawer at the right angle breaks the heavy paper. A flip of the wrist and the nickels pour into the register. Three rolls and the drawer's filled to the top. I've done this on early spring mornings and late summer days when the coins are hot to the touch. I've whacked the rolls on days when the heat fails to come on and it takes four or five hits until the paper tears and the coins tumble out.

In my day, I've seen millions of buffalos, staring at me from the face of the nickels. It's a peculiar variation of the American West, here at the skeeball center on the boardwalk, the buffalo devoid of meat and flesh, against the salty smell of the sand and the Atlantic Ocean. A herd of buffaloes stampeding into the crashing waves of the ocean.

I've been doing this so long, I can feel the weight of 20 coins without counting. One dollar's worth falls into the palm of my hand as if by some miracle, exactly the right number of nickels piled one on top of another.

The kids think I'm a genius. "Do that trick one more time," they tell me. Then they crowd around the register and watch as I scoop two handfuls of nickels into one of their hands. They count the coins slowly, hesitantly—18, 19, 20—and think that I'm a female Einstein. Only my hair that stands away from my head in every direction is dyed bright red and my eyeglass frames are pearly pink with rhinestones, not Einstein's square metal spectacles which I saw once in a picture in a Life magazine.

Do it again, they say almost every day. Some days I do the $2.00 trick, scooping out forty nickels without counting. They hoot and holler, and cheer me on, like one of the Second Avenue audiences from my theater days.

I wasn't doing coin tricks then. Just singing a couple of songs and cracking a few jokes to a straggly crowd who wandered in for the show. I was the warm-up act, paid $1.50 for my performance. I lived in a third-floor walk up tenement on Avenue A, near 5th Street. The bathroom was at the end of the hall and the stairway smelled of pee. But it was my home, the place I returned to when the show was over and I'd shrink back to my offstage identity, that of a poor, working girl in the big city.

Beverly Bridges, that was my stage name. But I was really Norma Beverly Bluestein, or at least that was the family name my grandmother had been given at Ellis Island when she arrived here with her four children in 1919. The real name was probably unpronounceable—something like Bluzinsky or Bluzinowitz. Some Polish name acquired in the shtetls of Eastern Europe, that when filtered through the eyes of the inspector at Ellis Island had become Bluestein, a nice American name that anyone, even someone with a third-grade education, could pronounce. My father became Marvin and when I was born, I was named Norma for his grandmother, Neche, who had died in her brick house before the Nazis marched the entire population of her village to a deserted field and shot them.

Nobody ever called me Norma. From as far back as I can remember, I was Beverly—Beverly this, and Beverly that. I remember signing my first library card, Beverly Bluestein in big square block letters and Beverly was the name on my report cards from P.S. 98, where I received three stars for elocution. Those stars were probably the reason why I fancied myself an actress, even at the age of 10. Whenever I had the chance, I would slip into the movie theater and watch the stars—their hair perfectly coiffed, their skin smooth and white, their voices sultry.

But you had to be born beautiful and I wasn't. I wasn't ugly, mind you. Not really ugly. No one said that I was ugly. I had thick brown hair that framed my face and needed desperately to be brushed every morning. My eyes were brown and deep-set but a little too small to be noticed. And I had a long neck that gave the impression that my head was a bit small for my body, that it was perched high in the air, somehow disconnected from my chest.

All in all that might have been fortuitous. In the era of boobs, I just didn't have any and no matter how much toilet paper I stuffed in my bra, I was as far from endowed as our East Broadway apartment was from Park Avenue. It didn't matter. I was funny. I could make people laugh, at me and at themselves.

"You ought to go on the stage" was what the butcher always said to me. For a new joke, he would put a few extra chicken legs into my package. He knew the man who owned the theater around the corner. One day, he handed me a slip of paper.

"I spoke to Victor about you yesterday," he said. "He wants to talk to you about a job."

Victor was the bald guy I passed daily. He stood under the marquee, smoking a cigar, watching the girls on their lunch hour. Victor appreciated good legs. You could tell that from the way he called to the girls who took their sandwiches to the park on sunny days. "Hey, sweetie, want a free ticket to see the show." I had a pretty good idea what Victor had in mind and it wasn't seeing the show. I was still a virgin, which probably made me all the more appealing to him. I had seen those movies where the young teenage girl gets drunk and sleeps with the older man. Not me. I wanted a young lover with a full head of hair. So, I folded up the slip of paper that the butcher had given me and shoved it in my jacket pocket.

One week later, I stopped by the theater and asked for him. I was wearing my navy dress with the polka dot sash and cuffs, the one that was copied from the dress that Betty Grable wore in Footlight Serenade. I had seen that movie twice and was thrilled when I found the dress in Macy's on the sale rack.

Victor looked me over and invited me into his office. It was on the mezzanine level, up one flight of stairs from the theater lobby. The place was a mess. Papers were piled on his desk and the only clear space was a small sofa, covered with a crocheted throw.

"Have a seat," he said to me, gesturing to the love seat. He pulled over his desk chair and sat opposite me, tapping his foot heavily on the wooden floor.

"I hear that you're funny and that you sing. At least that's what Sam said. I need someone to warm up the audience for the afternoon show. Tell me a few jokes." He puffed on his cigar and waited.

Within minutes, I gave him the one about the old lady and the plant and the mailman who was screwing the young widow—two of Sam's favorites. Victor laughed, loud and long. "You're hired," he said. "It's a Wednesday and Sunday matinee at 3 PM—$1.50 a performance.

I worked for Victor for years under my new name, Beverly Bridges. I had always loved bridges—they were magical, miracles. They carried heavy objects; they stood over the water. They were a way of getting from here to there.

Beverly Bridges was a much better name than Beverly Bluestein and to celebrate the change I dyed my hair red—not a sedate red but a bold Santa Claus red that shouted fake. When I walked on stage, the audience laughed, even before I began my shtick. Soon I was performing as a warm-up for the evening shows, too.

I didn't become famous though, although I did manage to get my friends free passes to the afternoon performance. The old man in the ticket booth was my buddy and he could be counted on to give me a loan to pay my bills. Victor knew nothing about our deal.

One day Victor called me into his office and told me that I was fired. "Don't take it personally," he said, which was one hell of a remark. "That's show business. The audience for live theater is changing. I've got an investor and I'm converting the theater to a movie house." He looked me in the face and I could see that he felt guilty.

"I know a guy who needs a manager," he said. "He runs a skeeball arcade out on the boardwalk. Give him a call and use my name."

So, before I knew it, I was the manager of Friedman's Skeeball Arcade on the boardwalk, with 20 alleys and a big following. It was a far cry from show business but I needed the job. The owner, Sol Friedman, came by every day to collect the cash and check that things were running smoothly. I was responsible for running the place. Friedman owned the building and he gave me a free apartment to live in on the floor above the arcade. Two little rooms with a kitchenette and a bathroom big enough for half a person. It was painted a dark green and the furniture looked like it was rejects from the thrift shop. The rent was great though—free.

I took over from Sophie, who had run the place for 20 years and was now slightly deaf.

At 70, Sophie had decided to retire. She was moving down to Miami, Florida, to live with her sister. There was a boardwalk down there, too. So, she figured, the adjustment would be easy.

"Sophie will fill you in on everything," Sol said to me on my first day on the job. "What she leaves out, I can tell you." He gave me a funny wink which made me feel squeamish. I'd have to keep the guy at a distance.

But Sophie wasn't feeling well on the day we were to meet and she went home early. The next morning she did not show up. The phone rang at 11:00 and it was Friedman. "I've got bad news for you," he said. "I just got a phone call from the hospital. Sophie had a heart attack and died. There goes her Miami retirement." He laughed a sort of forced laugh. Then, added, "I'll come by later, don't worry."

I sat on the tall, red stool by the cash register and surveyed the arcade. Half of the bulbs were burnt out. The winner sign was hanging askew. The red linoleum was dirty. The prize cabinet was half empty. Who knows when it had been restocked?

I was Beverly Bridges, the actress, the comedian. What was I doing here?

I looked into the mirror and saw a shocking head of red hair. I felt like crying but held back the tears. Crying was for sissies. Crying was for failures. But I felt like one, here on the boardwalk. By now, I should have been the star attraction on the playbill. I imagined myself on stage, teasing the audience, making them laugh.

No one would mistake me for the manager of an arcade. I opened the cash register and grabbed a handful of nickels, then walked over to alley number one and began to play. Ten points. Pretty sad. Twenty points—still not very good. Ten points again—pathetic. Zero points. Thirty points—getting better. Last ball, fifty points—triumphant at last.

For my nickel, I had rung up a score of 120 points. That was about right— the score of my life. Not impressive.

$1.50—that's 30 nickels. Two and one-half scoops and by magic I can dump 30 coins into the hand of a 10-year-old, eyeing the prizes on the shelves below the mirror: the fan with pictures of pagodas and the bisque kewpie dolls made in Japan, key rings and back scratchers, high bouncing rubber balls and shooter marbles in red, blue, and yellow.

For a nickel you got six wooden balls, six chances to score high points and win a prize. All you had to do was roll the ball up the alley and into the small center ring, the 50 points circle. Six winning rolls and you had 300 points, enough prize coupons to trade in for a set of four Eskimo kewpie dolls, two boys and two girls, dressed in native attire, their faces hand-painted. They were all smiling and they all had black hair.

Three hundred points more and you could take home a cap shooter that looked like the real thing, with spinning barrels and a leather holster. Or a miniature porcelain tea set, with six blue-and-white cups and saucers and a matching tea pot.

It was hard to roll six winning balls, though. More often than not, the balls flew into the outside ring, earning the thrower a mere ten points. The prizes for sixty points were grouped on the lowest rack, so the little kids could reach them, a pencil in iridescent pink, a plastic dinosaur about one inch long.

Sol Friedman had a wife who lived in Kew Gardens. Her name was Paula and he clearly no longer loved her. In fact, I soon learned, from Sol himself, that he loathed Paula. He had nothing good to say about her, except that she had given him two children, a son and a daughter, who weren't too bad considering the fact that she had given birth to them.

"How I spent years with that woman, I'll never know," he said to me nearly every time he saw me. "A complete nag. A woman who does not know how to laugh. She's the opposite of you."

I protested that everyone knows how to laugh and that my years as a comedian had taught me that it all depends on the jokes and the delivery, but Sol would not listen to me.

He reached over and took my hand. "You're wrong," he said. "Even the funniest joke, Jack Benny himself, could not make her laugh."

It was a friendly gesture, not a pass, although I was sure that Sol would have been willing to get into bed if I had been, but I wasn't. He was too old for me and too bald. I had my eyes on Arnold, the manager of the amusement park, who dropped by every day to play a few games and chat. Arnold was the divorced father of two and a frustrated stand-up comic. We used to trade jokes. That was promising. So far, it had all been words but there was a future with Arnold. There was none with Sol. I didn't tell him that. It would have hurt too much.

Sol often came by in the early evening, to sit across from me on a high stool and watch the kids play.

"Hey, you in number three," he said to Marty, a boy of 10 or so. "You're banking the ball wrong. Straighten your arm a bit just before you release it." Marty nodded and threw another ball. This time, it curved to the right, hit the side hard and then bounced into a 10 point ring.

"Too hard," Sol said. "I didn't tell you to throw it right. I said to curve it so it hits and then bounces back dead center."

I watched Marty throw a second ball. It flew through the air, curved to the right, hit lightly and then fell into the middle circle for fifty points. The kid jumped up and down and screamed, then, turned to Sol and made the thumbs up sign.

"What'd I tell you?" Sol said. "Some people listen to me when I speak," Sol continued. "Not Paula. She does the opposite. If I say chicken for dinner, it's fish. If I want to go out dancing, it's staying at home watching the television. That woman drives me crazy. You're lucky, Beverly, smart that you stayed single. You don't have to argue with anybody. You just do what you want to do and that's that."

I laughed when he said that. After all, living alone wasn't as great as he thought it to be.

"I've no one to take care of me," I said. "No one. If I'm sick, it's just me. If I'm hungry and there's nothing in the house, I have to get food. If I feel like conversation, I talk to myself. It's freedom at a price." I didn't say a word about Arnold.

"Worth it," Sol said. "I'd pay anything for it. Anything."

His face was serious and I could see that he meant what he was saying. "All of the immigrants come to America for freedom," he said, "me, I'm stuck." Sol opened up the cash register and took out a handful of nickels. He walked over to alley nine, his favorite, and began to play. Ball one—fifty points. The ball flew through the air, hit the side, and then slipped into the smallest circle.

He turned to look at me, waiting for my applause.

"Not bad," I said. "You should try out for the Yankees."

Sol laughed and threw the second ball. It hit the left, then magically curved back dead center to squeeze into the fifties circle.

"See, I'm ambidextrous," he said. "Whew! Didn't think I was going to make it that time." He mopped his forehead with a large white handkerchief that sported an SMF monogram in large capital letters. M was for Melvin.

I had seen him go through this routine a hundred times. Nine times out of ten, he scored a perfect game. The man was a genius, a skeeball genius. That's how he got into the business in the first place. Or at least that was the story he told.

He met a guy at the track who owned the skeeball arcade and invited Sol over to play. The guy prided himself on his being the best player in the east. Sol took him on. One day, in the heat of passion, the guy bet the arcade.

It was a big mistake. Sol won the wager, beating him 20 games straight.

He took over the arcade and expanded it, buying out the lease of the adjacent jewelry store. He hired a local carpenter and doubled the number of alleys and he paid a local artist to design a new sign—a three-dimensional work with four moving balls. The balls moved from left to right across the blue backdrop, falling into a hole marked 50 points. The sign was the talk of the boardwalk. On the first day it was up, hundreds of spectators gathered in front of the arcade and the local newspaper sent a reporter and a cameraman to cover the story.

"The boardwalk needs new life," Sol told the reporter. "I decided to give it a shot in the arm." Friedman stood side by side with the artist, Jonathan Kamen, who turned the switch and set the balls in motion.

Sol kept a framed clipping of the story on the wall behind the cash register, a yellowing reminder of that moment of triumph.

"I'm the only one alive," Sol told me one day, pointing to the old picture. "Kamen died young and the mayor died last year. I've outlived them all." He chuckled and then went back to complaining about Paula. They'd had a big fight the night before and Sol had spent the night on the canvas cot in the back room of the arcade.

"What do you think I should do?" he asked me.

"About what?" I answered.

"About Paula. Should I leave her for good?"

At least once a week, I faced the same question. Should he leave? What should he do?

I never knew what to answer him. "Don't know," I said. "Remember, I've never been married."

I stood by the prize case and counted the kewpie dolls. I was running low on the Asian dolls. They were the most popular, two-to-one. Three cowgirl dolls remained. No one wanted them. I placed them in a box and dusted the cabinet.

"It's time for another prize order," I said. Sol bought the prizes from a friend in Brooklyn, who bought them from another friend, who dealt with an import-export firm in Manhattan. They all played poker on Wednesday nights.

I took out a sheet of ruled paper and began making a list: three dozen Asian kewpies, a dozen ball-and-jacks sets, 100 shooter marbles, 50 folding fans with pictures of gondolas on the canals of Venice, a huge stuffed giraffe (for 10,000 points), 20 makeup kits (for 1,000 points each), and two radios (for 15,000).

Sol stood up and looked over my shoulder. "How many radios did we give away last year?" he asked.

I had to think for a minute or two. I remembered the grey and pink radio that Susan had claimed only a few weeks ago. She was a regular at the arcade, coming in four or five afternoons a week. "Don't give away my radio," she said, every time she left. Then, she appeared with a knapsack full of coupons.

"15,004," she said, "enough for my radio and two pieces of bubble gum." She laughed at her arithmetic and I climbed up on the ladder and retrieved her radio. It needed a dusting and a cleaning. But when I was through, it was adorable—a bedroom Zenith portable with a tiny motif of a poodle in one corner.

"Cutest radio I've ever seen," I said, wrapping it in tissue.

The only other radio we had given away last year was a dark brown one, with oversize dials. The winner was Chuck, who worked as a mechanic at the garage about a mile away. He and his girlfriend were regulars at the arcade and they squabbled over how to redeem their 16,000 points. Shirley wanted the stuffed giraffe but that would only leave 6,000 points left—not enough for the radio. In the end, Chuck talked her into the radio, winning her over with one of the makeup kits.

Sol was still waiting for my answer.

"Two radios. We gave away two radios last year," I said.

"Order a half dozen for next year," he said. "And double the order of kewpie dolls."

I started to protest but could see from the look on his face that he had made up his mind, although I couldn't figure out why. Business was slower these days, especially in the summer—our high season. We were losing customers to the beach clubs, where the ladies played canasta and the gentlemen gin rummy. The kids were in day camp. The regulars seemed to be dwindling.

There's no point arguing with the boss. Not if the boss was Sol. Not if Sol was in a foul mood about Paula. So I put down his order and handed him the paper. He read my list, then took the pencil from my hand and added a few more items: two dozen magic kits, 50 high bouncing Spaldings, pink and blue flashlights.

It was our biggest order ever and Sol smiled when he read the final list. Then, he folded the paper in a small square and slipped it into his shirt pocket.

"Consider it done," he said to me. He put on his plaid sports jacket, made a final check of the cash register and went to his back office for a moment.

"See you Thursday," he said to me with a wave. He started to walk away and then came back to tell me one more thing. "I never tell you how good you are, Beverly," he said. "I couldn't run this place without you."

It was a funny, sentimental moment from a gruff guy and I nodded in response. Words just didn't come to me. I knew he meant it but you just can't start being emotional with someone all of a sudden. It doesn't work that way.

Fifteen minutes after Sol left, the arcade filled up. Ten Boy Scouts with their troop leader on an outing. Six seniors, all canasta buddies, who lived in the hotel 100 feet down the boardwalk. Esther was their leader and she fancied herself my best friend.

"You're looking glum, Beverly," she said. "What's wrong?"

Esther could read your heart. I was feeling down. Arnold hadn't been around for two days. I hadn't been able to trade jokes with anyone. For the past week, I had spent most of my time removing wads of gum from the wooden panels on the skeeball games and polishing the glass prize case. Sitting on my perch, I could watch the kids studying the prizes and catch the shoplifters. "I promise never to do it again," they always said to me when I threatened to turn them in.

I was so down that I didn't audition for the local variety show that was held every year in the town auditorium. They loved my Elvis impersonation, the crowd of senior citizens and the local battalion from the Knights of Columbus, struggling to their feet to applaud my singing and gyrations.

There was talk of a talent scout coming but no one showed up. Afterwards, I signed programs for twenty deaf old ladies and walked back to the arcade in the cold, skipping the post-performance pizza party. I just wasn't in the mood.

Esther was waiting for me to speak. "Guess you're right," I said. "I am feeling sad." I thought about telling her the one about the mother duck but she had already joined her friends at alley six.

Arnold showed up just as the Scouts were leaving. They were clustered around the prize case, fighting over who was going to get the last shooter marble. I had my hands full making peace, offering, as a compromise, a three-coupon jack set to placate the kid who lost the toss over the marble.

"It's a much better prize," I whispered to him, using my best theatrical voice. "That marble isn't very good. This is the best jack set they make. The ball's a real high bouncer." I squeezed his hand and prayed. He took my offering and winked. We had cut a deal.

Arnold watched the negotiating from ten feet back and I heard him laugh.

"You haven't lost your touch, Beverly," he said. "It's all show business. You sure know how to work the crowd."

Arnold was carrying a brown paper bag which he set down on the counter by the cash register. "I brought you dinner," he said. He lifted two hot dogs out of the bag, followed by a large paper container of french fries and two Pepsis. "Hope you like the works," he said, handing me my frank, smothered with sauerkraut and mustard.

Arnold placed a french fry in his right hand and closed his fist. Then, he rotated both hands in the air.

"Which hand has the french fry?" Arnold asked me. In his show biz days, Arnold told a few jokes and did magic—mostly at birthday parties.

I touched his left hand and he opened it. It was empty.

"Gotta keep your eyes open," he said, giving me a huge smile.

I reached into the drawer and took out two nickels. "I've got one for you," I said, placing the nickels in my left fist. "Which hand has the nickels," I asked Arnold. I could tell from the look on his face that he knew the answer. But he played along.

"That one," he said, pointing to my right fist.

I opened my right fist and it was empty. Then, I opened my left. It was empty too.

"Here they are," I said, reaching into my jacket pocket.

"Not bad, for an amateur," Arnold said. "But don't give up your day job."

His wisecrack brought me back to reality. "My day job's not much to hold on to," I said, "especially these days. The kids who come don't hang around for my jokes. They've got better things to do. And the old timers–they want to tell me their stories. Not listen to mine."

Arnold was sympathetic. Attendance in the amusement park was dwindling too. "We hit our lowest number ever last week," he said. "The only ride that was full was the whip." Arnold threw a french fry up in the air and tried to catch it with his teeth. The fry landed on top of the cash register, wedged between the eight and the nine keys.

"I'm like an aged seal," Arnold said, "I just keep missing my cue."

"Me, too," I said, twirling my last fry in the air.

On Thursday morning, Sol showed up earlier than usual.

"I put in our order last night," he said. "Maury will have it by Tuesday, at the latest. Can you wait?"

"Sure," I said. Then, gathering my courage, I added, "Business has been slow, you know Sol. I'm a little worried."

"Nothing to worry about," he said. "I had my palm read Tuesday and the gypsy told me that next year business would be booming. That's why I placed such a big order for prizes. She predicted that I would leave Paula. I've been thinking about it for two days. How am I ever going to have the courage to make that move?"

"I'm not an expert on courage," I told Sol. "If I was, I'd still be trying to make it in show business. I wouldn't be managing this arcade if I knew how to say I quit. Don't get me wrong. You're good to me and I appreciate the job. But it's pretty far from Broadway."

Sol nodded his head in agreement. I knew that he understood. I mean here we were day after day, week after week, sitting in the arcade with the peeling sign and the prizes lined up in the glass case, both of us waiting for a miracle.

Sol reached into his worn leather briefcase and handed me a sealed envelope.

"Put this in the cash register drawer," he said. "I don't want to leave it around my house."

I wanted to ask him what was in it but his face said, don't ask, so I didn't. It was something he didn't want Paula to find. He was always telling me how she opened his mail. I walked over to the register, unlocked the drawer and placed the envelope inside.

"Whatever it is, it's safe here," I said.

After he left, I locked up the arcade and walked home. It was about a year since I had moved out of the apartment over the arcade, finding it small and drafty. I now lived two blocks away on the second floor of a garden apartment building. I opened a can of tuna fish, washed some lettuce and toasted two pieces of rye bread. I sat down to finish the mystery that I had started several weeks earlier. I was sure that the rich widow was guilty but discovered on page 190 that she was really innocent. Who, then, had murdered the company president? I fell asleep reading, waking in time to wash up and watch the evening news.

The static on my television set was worse than usual. Thirty seconds of international news. Russia was censoring the United States and Cold War tensions were building. A quick shift to local trouble. A nude woman had been found murdered in Central Park. Two children were killed in a tenement fire in

Queens. They showed their Confirmation pictures on the screen.

Before the weather came on, there was another sad item to report, said the announcer, reading from a piece of paper that had just been handed to him: "Skeeball entrepreneur Sol Friedman was found dead this evening. His body was slumped over the steering wheel of his Cadillac." There was a photo of Sol, taken perhaps five years ago, standing in front of the arcade, waving to the camera. I was in the photo, too, slightly to the left of the entrance, leaning against the metal gate. I couldn't believe the news. I had seen Sol a few hours ago. We had talked about the gypsy's reading.

It had to have been an accident. Or maybe he'd been murdered. But who would have wanted to murder Sol? One thing I was certain about, Sol would never have killed himself. Not Sol, the man who had just filled out his biggest prize list—more radios than he could give away in a year. Pink radios and green radios. Black-and-white-checked radios. Kewpie dolls with slanting eyes and red lips. Giraffes with plush fur and long eyelashes. Hundreds of treasures for the roll of a ball. Only a nickel to win. Thousands of orange coupons with his name printed on them in bold black letters: Friedman's Skeeball Arcade. Best Gifts in New York.

I got dressed and returned to the arcade. At night the place smelled of sea and mildew. I opened the metal gate, removed the padlock and entered. There was a scurrying sound—probably of a field mouse retreating to his hole in the wall, then silence. I put on the light and walked over to the register.

I opened the locked drawer and took out the envelope. Carefully, with my letter opener, I opened the envelope. Inside was a handwritten note from Sol, written in black ink, his letters full of strange swirls.

"Dear Beverly," he wrote. "You are the only one who loved the skeeball arcade as much as I did. Paula always wanted me to sell it. Jeffrey and Carol hated the place. That's why I'm leaving it to you, free and clear, with enough cash in the bank to keep those wooden balls rolling up the alleys.

"You made me laugh. Love, Sol."

I slipped the note in my jacket pocket, locked the gate and walked down the creaky wooden steps from the boardwalk to the beach below. The tide was receding, each wave falling short of the one before. Fiddler crabs chased one another on the sand, leaving their strange triangular markings. I reached down and grabbed a handful of wet seaweed and began popping the green bubbles between my thumb and forefinger as I walked west.

Playworld

July 1958

THE PAGE WAS DOG-EARED and starting to fray at the corners—a stark, black-and-white photograph of the Ferris wheel at the 1893 Chicago World's Fair, designed by engineer, George W.G. Ferris, 1859-1896. Ferris was a genius.

I took a deep breath and looked at my Ferris wheel, the tallest ride in Playworld, the one that the children loved and feared. It was about 40 feet high, towering above the other rides, the toy trains that chugged slowly around the rusted tracks, the motor boats that made circles in the dirty water, the carousel with its white and gold ponies, and the bumper cars, where the blue, yellow, and red cars crashed into one another. Bang. Bang.

Those were a favorite of the boys who pretended that they were their fathers, tough-talking men whose white shirtsleeves were rolled up to their elbows. When you got behind the wheel of a car, there was no time for cowardice. You had to be aggressive or you would die in a fiery collision, your car a burning heap of twisted metal.

I was always warning them to keep their hands inside the swinging cages of the Ferris wheel but they didn't listen. Instead, they stuck out their tongues and laughed, "Nothing to worry about, Arnold," they said. "Give us more juice!" I knew that they wanted me to push the black lever up to high, to make them spin mercilessly out of control. But I never did it. It was too dangerous. There was no telling whether the nuts and bolts that I tightened every week would withstand the strain of the centrifugal force, the energy that would send the cages careening over the fence into the crowd of bystanders, mothers, fathers, sisters, and brothers, their hands sticky from jelly apples and cotton candy.

I kept my gloved hand on the throttle, holding a middle course while the boys taunted me. "C'mon, Arnold," they said. "Let 'er rip!" For a moment, I imagined that I was a space man, the sleek figure dressed in a white suit, who was the hero of the comics. Like the kids, I was addicted to them, spending my lunch hour flipping through the pages while I ate my sandwich on a bench on the boardwalk.

It was a wild idea—this walking in space or landing on the moon. Positively thrilling. I would pack three changes of clothing, a photo of Beverly, and a couple dozen Mars bars just in case my food supply ran out. When I stood before the control panel of the Ferris wheel, my mind wandered. I imagined red blinking lights and square white buttons: liftoff, descent, and landing, all in capital letters. At the top, there was a large orange button marked EMER-GENCY.

In fact, the Ferris wheel had an on-and-off toggle switch, a red warning light and the throttle. I'd wipe my brow with a red bandana that I wore knotted around my neck. Then, I'd flip the switch and inch the throttle forward, slowly and steadily. The steel cages rocked back and forth in the air, as the wheel began to turn and the children screamed. The wheel began to spin and Peter, a blonde-haired kid with a green-and-white-striped T-shirt, began to wave furiously, leaning out of the cage to scream, "Look at me, look at me," to his younger brother below.

"Stop that," I would scream back at Peter. "Get your hand back inside the car. No waving and no standing up!" My voice could be heard across Playworld. Beverly said that sometimes she could even hear me inside the arcade on the boardwalk. "You don't need a megaphone, Arnold" she said, with a laugh.

By late afternoon, I was hoarse from trying to contain the kids, with the notable exception of a skinny brown-haired boy of about twelve, who stood by the rail and watched. He was always alone and he never talked to anyone. One day, I asked him his name. His eyes were startled and he hesitated before he answered.

"Joey," he said, not offering one word more.

"Want to give me a hand?" I asked him. "I've got a zillion pennies that need to be rolled. I'll pay you a quarter an hour and I'll throw in free rides on the Ferris wheel."

"I can only work until 2:00 PM." Joey said, "If that's OK with you. I'll take the quarter. Forget the free rides."

We had struck our little deal. Every day around noon, Joey showed up with his peanut butter and jelly sandwich and his ragged Yankees baseball cap which he'd tip at me, instead of saying hello. I led him into my office and sat him down at the wooden desk, stained with oil and grease. Then, I'd dump a mound of pennies in front of him and hand him a stack of red rolling papers, which were to be filled 50 to a roll.

"I'm good at math," Joey said. "Not as good as Martha, who can add, subtract, multiply, and divide in her head. But pretty good. Try me."

"Four times eight plus seven minus nine," I said, barely able to catch my breath.

"Thirty," he answered, a big smile on his face.

Joey was a terrific little worker. Nothing distracted him, not even the screams of the other kids on the wheel. Not even their taunts. "Fraidy cat! Fraidy Cat! Hey you, you're a fraidy cat!" They could see him hunched over the desk, counting.

Joey never looked up. He counted his pennies out loud, "45, 46, 47, 48, 49, 50." Then, he started again.

When I looked at his face, I could see that he was mesmerized by the coins, lost within himself, as if I he were in a dark cave, far from the light. The screaming children on the Ferris wheel had little effect on him. Their taunts, their shrieks were nothing. He had entered a private space where only he had the key. Try as I did to reach out to him, he remained withdrawn.

Until one Thursday, when he appeared at Playworld with a small green knapsack on his back, his hair slightly disheveled, and his face agitated. He threw the backpack on the floor of my office and sat down at the desk, lowering his head on his hands. I could hear him crying. I stood at the door, hoping that he'd look up and see me, but he didn't.

Finally, after more than a half hour, I called to him, "Joey, can I help you? What's wrong?" At first, he merely shook his head, as if to say nothing. After a few minutes, he looked up at me and spoke, "I can't live there any more," he said. Then he began to cry all over again. I put my arm around his shoulder and drew him close to me. I was an only child and my own father never had any time to hug me. He worked from morning to night as a plumber. When he got home, there was dinner, the news on TV, and bed.

I knew that he loved me, though. And so did my mother, who worked as a seamstress. They just didn't have time to show it. I stood there, thinking about them, as I hugged Joey. Poor kid.

Beverly would be better at comforting him, I thought. She would cradle him in her arms and sing him a song or tell him a funny story that would dry up his tears. "Can't be that bad, whatever it is," I said. "Things always seem worse than they actually are."

I was thinking about my business at the amusement park. Attendance was down and I wasn't sure why. Beverly thought it was because of television. The kids were sitting indoors glued to the screen. How, she said, could I compete with Howdy Doody? I thought she was wrong. Nothing could compete with the thrill of the Ferris wheel—rotating in the air, defying gravity, smelling the salt of the sea, looking down as the waves crashed onto the beach.

I was scared. The day would come when I'd have to shut down the wheel and go to work in an office. "I've got things that I'm afraid of too, Joey," I said. "Things that make me sad."

Joey stopped crying and looked up at me. His look said, you too. His face was swollen from crying and his eyes were very red.

"I've run away from the orphanage," he said, "and I'm never going back. Never."

For the moment, I was stunned. I had assumed that Joey lived in one of the bungalows near the beach, with his family and a big dog. I'd never thought of the orphanage, the stucco building five blocks east and one block from the ocean. It had been there for fifty years and was funded by six or seven charities including the Ladies' League and the Knights of Columbus. Once a year, the orphans were transported to Playworld in yellow school buses for a day at the amusement park. The kids were given tickets for a dozen rides and food vouchers, too. Beverly always gave them extra prizes in the skeeball arcade, without coupons. I let them ride on the Ferris wheel for free. There was something canned about their laughter, artificially produced to please their teachers and the orphanage directors.

It was please, sir, this, and please, sir, that, plaintive little voices, heads bowed, to avoid your gaze. I always felt uncomfortable in their presence, guilty because I had had two parents and four grandparents.

Joey had fooled me. In a million years, I would never have picked him out as an orphan. I had missed that lonely, longing look on Joey's face. He was a very good actor, that kid, a miniature Rock Hudson.

"Let me live with you," Joey pleaded, pulling on my flannel shirt. "Tell them, you're going to adopt me."

There was this desperate look on his face. Don't return me to that awful place, his eyes said. Have pity. For a moment, I imagined myself cooking spaghetti for Joey. He was sitting on my green kitchen chair, watching as I stirred the pasta. Beverly was chopping garlic for the sauce. We were the quintessential American family: mother, father, and child. The light from the setting sun bounced off the freshly waxed kitchen floor.

Joey was smiling at me. After a moment, he began to whistle, "She'll Be Coming Round the Mountain When She Comes." Beverly joined in for the refrain. The image blurred, then faded away. The little boy before me was waiting for my answer.

"I live alone now," I said, as if to soften the answer that I was about to give him. I didn't mention Beverly, who had her own place but who often stayed with me. "I never go home, you know. I spend my days and my nights here, too. I don't have a life of my own. I only get to see my kids every couple of weeks and they live 45 minutes away." It all poured out. I was baring my soul to this kid who I hardly knew. And, while I was talking, I was looking into his sad eyes and asking myself, why not?

My son, Robert, was seven but he was definitely his mother's boy. It had been years since he laughed at my jokes. "Give me a break, Dad," he was always telling me, "those jokes are old. Nobody would laugh at them." I didn't even try to answer him. When I saw him every other Saturday night, we went to the movies, his choice, and ate Chinese food, most of the time in silence.

Pamela was a little better. She had just turned nine and she loved bright pink lipstick and glittery nail polish. She still liked to ride on the Ferris wheel and she thought that I was important because I was The Boss at the amusement park. Most important of all, Pamela loved my jokes. "Tell those rabbit jokes again, dad," she would beg. "Question: How does the Easter Bunny stay healthy? Answer: He does eggsercise. Question: How does a rabbit look like a cornstalk? Answer: They both have big ears!" Pamela would roll on the ground, holding her sides to prevent herself from splitting apart. But Pamela was under her mother's control and my visits with her were strictly regulated.

Joey could be my own kid, the child I did not have to share, the perfect audience for my comedy routine. I could try out my jokes on him and practice my magic. He could hold the black hat when I pulled the rabbit out, or feel behind my ear for the missing coin.

"You can't just run away," I said to Joey. "You have to return."

Joey shook his head and did not look at me. I wanted him to plead with me. But he had shut down.

"So it's goodbye, then," he said. He started to leave but I put my hand on his shoulder to stop him.

"I'm not promising you anything," I said, "but I'm not saying no either."

Joey gave me a big hug, tighter than I had ever been hugged before. It was a save-my-life-have-pity-on-me hug. It was a don't-mess-up-my-life-is-depending-on-you hug. I was in big trouble now. I had sort of promised the kid that he could live with me. I wasn't even sure that I could get permission and I didn't how my kids and Beverly would react.

After I closed up that night, I walked by the skeeball arcade. Beverly was pulling the metal gate across the front of the store and I helped her lock up.

"You look awful, Arnold," she said, glancing up at my face. "Who dropped the bomb on you?"

There was no fooling Beverly. "A kid named Joey, the boy who's been hanging around the park. Turns out he's from the orphanage. Today, he asked me to let him live with me." My voice trembled as I said that last line. Beverly looked stunned.

"You let him down gently, I suppose," she said. "No point hurting a kid." She avoided my eyes, choosing instead to rub at a spot on the sleeve of her blouse. As far as I could tell, there was nothing to rub out.

"Actually, I didn't say no. I sort of told him that I would look into it. That was the least I could do. Poor kid, he's miserable. Who'd want to live in that place? Smells when you walk past it. All of the kids have runny noses. You feel sorry for those kids, too."

"True," said Beverly. "But that doesn't mean that I want one of them to live with me. You have two kids of your own who you hardly see."

We walked side by side on the boardwalk. Most of the stalls were shuttered for the night. You could hear the waves splashing on the sand and smell the salt air. I put my arm around Beverly's shoulder and felt her shiver. She leaned against me for a second, then reached out for my hand.

"You're sweet, Arnold," she said. "Sweet as cotton candy."

We both laughed and inadvertently licked our lips, searching for the sticky residue. Nothing could be sweeter than spun pink sugar. I understood that this was Beverly's way of saying that I was a sucker for a sad kid who needed a home.

"Think I'll go by the orphanage and speak to the director," I said. Beverly squeezed my hand. It felt like a squeeze of approval. We stopped for a bite to eat at the luncheonette. The special was cold red borscht and we ordered two large bowls with pumpernickel bread.

"Hold the sour cream," Beverly said to Carol, the red-haired waitress who always took care of us. "And put in some extra beets, last time I could hardly find any."

"That's cause you need new glasses," Carol quipped. "I'll be happy to loan you mine! You, too, Arnold. What's your beef?"

"Have none today, Carol," I said. "Not yet." I usually joked around with her but the conversation about Joey had turned me serious.

"Ran out of jokes today," I told Carol. "Running on empty."

"Half-empty," she said. "It's just a little dry spell. By the time I return with your order, you'll have a new one."

But I didn't. The truth was that I was obsessing about Joey and the orphanage. The whole thing was crazy. My business was bad. Playworld was rotting away. What I needed to do was to concentrate on turning things around financially and on making a life with Beverly.

After a half hour, Carol came by to hand us the check. "You must be sick," she said, picking up my still full soup bowl. "Sick or in love," she said as she slid her wet rag across the Formica table top and pressed the check to the wet surface.

"It's on me," said Beverly, grabbing the check. She reached into her dark brown imitation snakeskin purse and pulled out two dollars. "Keep the change," she said to Carol.

The next morning, I walked over to the orphanage before opening the park. The stucco building needed repair. There were deep cracks in the wall and several of the first-floor windows were broken. Two of the front steps were missing bricks. I rang the bell three times. On the last ring, a woman in a grey shirtwaist dress opened the door.

"Can I help you?" she said, annoyed to be disturbed. It was the kind of voice that could line kids up, however unruly. I imagined her dangling Joey in the air by his collar or pinching his ear mercilessly when he disobeyed.

"I'm Arnold Gherman," I said, doing my best to be charming. "I'm the manager of Playworld, on the boardwalk. I'd like to talk to the director."

"That would be me," she said, even more curtly. It was obvious that I had committed a cardinal sin in thinking her some petty functionary. "And what would you like to see the director about?" she asked, her face stony and expressionless.

"Joey Gibbons," I replied.

"What did he do wrong now?" she asked, her brows arched and her lips pursed. "That kid is always getting in trouble. No matter how I punish him, he won't listen."

"Nothing," I said. She was a tough woman, mean and scary. "I need help at the amusement park and I thought that Joey might be the right kid for the job. I've talked to him a couple times and I think that we would get along." I knew better than to say that he was already a daily fixture at the park

She perked up. "I didn't mean to suggest that Joey's a bad kid," she said. She was warming to the idea of getting Joey off her hands. "Like all boys, he's just a bit rebellious. It's a great idea. Perhaps you'd like to tell him yourself."

She invited me in. We walked through the drab waiting room to a stairway. "Joey's is on the first door on the right on the second floor," she said, leading the way. We walked up the stairs, the gray carpet frayed and dirty. The hallway smelled of stale food.

She knocked on Joey's door and waited. Within a few seconds, he opened the door, looking smaller than he seemed when I saw him at the park.

"This is Mr. Arnold Gherman," she said, "the manager of Playworld. We've spoken and I think that you should work for him." She shook my hand and left the room.

Joey was afraid to speak. I sat down on his bed. It was very narrow, and the mattress was hard. He obviously shared the room with another boy because there was a matching cot on the other side. There was also a wooden desk with two chairs. I stared at the desk in disbelief. Sitting dead center on the desk, taking up three-quarters of its area, was a cardboard model of Playworld. The Ferris wheel. The race cars. The trains with the coal and lumber cars. The rides constructed out of pieces of cardboard and glued and taped together. The Ferris wheel was painted silver. The racing cars were red and yellow. There was even a cardboard figure of me, standing by my office. Next to me was the figure of a small boy—his hand swinging in mid-air.

There were green benches and there was a big sign by the entrance, printed in the same square orange letters as the actual sign: Playworld: A Place for Fun and Fantasy.

"How long did it take you to build this?" I asked Joey, as I fingered one of the cars. I noticed that there were yellow checked cushions on the red seats, exactly like the ones on the ride.

"The trickiest part was the cages on the Ferris wheel," Joey said. "I've been working on those for a year. It took me a while to figure out how to use paper clips to make them swing back and forth."

Joey stood up and walked over to his creation. His back was to me. He turned so that I could see what he had done. The boy's hand was joined with the man's.

The Prize

Summer 1958

I HAD NOT SEEN ARNOLD for over a week. The last time we were together we'd cleaned and polished the bumper cars, washing them with soapy water and applying Simonize. It took a dozen T-shirts torn into rags and ten hours of hard labor to make the red and blue cars shine.

Arnold paid me to scrape wads of chewing gum from the backs and undersides of the seats and from the plastic upholstery. It was tricky work. The knife could gash the fabric, if you were not careful.

"Slide it this way," Arnold said, as he demonstrated his prying technique. The pink wad of gum became loose in a second, flying through the air and landing on the trampled grass that surrounded the ride. He handed me the knife. My hand shook. The last time I used a knife, I ended up in the emergency room of the hospital with a deep gash that would not stop bleeding. I was tying up bundles of newspapers and the knife slipped when I tried to cut the twine. I screamed and Arnold bundled me into his car. We raced to the hospital, going through two red lights. I kept moaning that I was sorry.

"Don't apologize," Arnold said.

I turned the knife sideways and slid the blade under the edge of the gum.

"Do it slowly," Arnold said, patting me on the back. I loved that pat. His hand was large and warm—caressing my shoulder. No one else ever did that. At least, no one I remembered. I'd been living in the orphanage since I was three years old. My mother had abandoned me in the playground for toddlers, next door to the Methodist Church. There is a photo of me documenting my arrival. I am dressed in a blue sailor suit with a red bow tie. My brown hair is parted neatly. Someone clearly loved me, or at the very least someone took very good care of me. But no one ever claimed me. For years, I insisted that my mother's name was Cora. The police tried to find her. They checked all of the records. But there was only one Cora, Cora Vincent Bell, a frail woman of 80 who lived

82

in The Ocean Breeze nursing home.

At the orphanage, I was always in trouble. I wet my bed until I was five. As a punishment, they made me sleep in my wet sheets. I got into fistfights with the other boys, who drenched me with water balloons while I was sleeping and called me stupid. To get back at them, I stole pencils from their lockers and hid their baseball caps. I was always being punished for bad behavior—confined to my room for talking at assembly, assigned extra dishwashing duty for failing to turn out my nightlight at 10 PM. There was just no way I could ever be good.

Good was Caroline who curtsied when Mrs. Hutchinson walked by and crossed herself twice when a black cat darted in front of her. Caroline got two helpings of ice cream and Mrs. H's hand-me-down white blouses. They hung on her bony frame, their lace-trimmed collars two sizes too big for her skinny neck. I hated Caroline. I would have pushed her off a cliff if there was one in our sea-level city. One night I dreamed of drowning her in the Atlantic Ocean. She was screaming for me to rescue her and I was just standing there, sticking out my tongue and laughing as she was sucked out to sea. Take that, you snitch. You rat. You just want me to suffer.

Caroline was always taunting me. "Saw you at Playworld," she yelled at me one day in the crowded cafeteria, making sure that everyone could hear her. I caught my milk container as it was about to slide off the tray. Playworld was off limits and the kids were jealous because I had special permission to work there. Arnold had convinced Mrs. H that working there would set me straight.

"Saw you with Arnold," she said, sneering at me. "You were sweeping his sidewalk."

I swept Arnold's sidewalks twice a week, weeded his grass, too. In fact, I did everything Arnold asked me to do. Why not? Arnold was the only one who loved me. He was going to adopt me, too—as soon as Beverly said yes. All I had to do was convince her that we would all be better off as a threesome.

That would be tricky. When I stopped by the skeeball arcade, there was no hug and no kiss. She'd pour a handful of nickels into a red plastic bowl and shove it in my face. "Show me your stuff," she'd say.

I'd imitate Arnold, pacing back and forth before I released the ball, holding my breath as it curved toward the center. Arnold made noise when he played. "You can do it," he would yell at the ball. "Don't disappoint me."

My ball hit the rim and bounced into the gutter. I turned my back to Beverly because I didn't want her to see that I was about to cry.

"Put a little more spin on it," Beverly said, demonstrating with a twist of her right wrist.

I tried again, desperate to get the ball to land in the center hole. Maybe if I did that, she would love me as much as Arnold did. But it bounced out again. Beverly returned to counting coins and, after a half hour or so of defeat, I walked back to the orphanage.

With Arnold, things were different. He was rooting for me and I knew it.

A wad of green gum flew into the air. Arnold clapped. "Atta boy!" he said.

"A chip off the old block," he said. We worked side by side, sharing a tall Coke and a bag of chips.

"Beverly's making dinner Thursday night and she'd like you to come." I knew that it was Arnold who really wanted me to come but it was sweet of him to lie. Sweet of him to make me feel good.

I needed to ask permission for a night out. There was a form that Arnold would have to sign. Mrs. Hutchinson would have to agree and stamp it and I would have to return by 10 PM sharp, or else I would lose my visiting privileges for two months. I had slipped up once, arriving back at the orphanage at 10:03 to find her waiting for me in the lobby.

"I'll meet you at the greyhound arcade at 7 PM. We can play a few games and then go home for dinner." Arnold loved the dog races in Florida where the hounds streaked around the track panting, as their owners screamed from the stands.

I had only seen the arcade with the mechanical dogs. But Arnold's stories about the dog track filled my imagination. They were more than dogs, these legendary creatures who could run 45 mph, chasing an artificial hare around the track. Sweating profusely as they ran, they were cheered on by millions of working-class men. In 1946, just one year after World War II ended, some 34 million paying spectators went to the track to bet on the dogs.

They had names like Blue Wind and Victory and Lightning and they didn't live very long, three or four years of fame, followed by an early death. Grey at birth, there was no time to grow old.

At the arcade, the dogs did not sweat and they did not die. They were made of cast metal, painted dark grey, with blue eyes. They were all identical, with the exception of the numbers on their back, which were printed on squares of white, surrounded by red and yellow and green and purple. I always played number 12. Twelve was my lucky number, the age I would be when

Arnold adopted me. My birthday was coming up and I would be eleven which did not give me much time.

All you had to do was hit the handle, which hit the ball, which landed in the right box, which made the dog inch up the fake green grass track to victory. You had to be fast and steady, and work up a sweat and a rhythm. And you had to focus on your dog and your dog alone.

Mrs. H signed the form with one comment, "Ten o'clock," she said.

Arnold showed up ten minutes late.

"Hard to close up," he said, bending down to give me a kiss on the cheek. There were six players ready to go. The bell rang and the dogs were off, clicking their way upward.

"Four is going to win," Arnold whispered to me.

A college age kid was playing 4, his hand deftly hitting the handle. He leaned into the track, his blonde hair hanging over his face.

The player to his right, 7, was giving him a good fight. But he kept coughing and you could see that he was getting tired. Stamina. That's what you needed to win and he clearly did not have enough.

Arnold poked me in the ribs and pointed to him. "Going down," he said. "Second or third place."

Suddenly, there was a burst of energy from the woman on the end. One was moving up, about to pass 7.

"Atta boy, atta boy," she shouted as her dog lurched forward.

"Second place," Arnold said to me, as he nodded to her.

The bell rang. Arnold was right on the money, as usual. First, Second, and Third.

Betty was busy giving out prizes to the winners as Arnold and I lined up to play. He chose 8. I decided to play 11. Placing her trophy, a stuffed giraffe, on the ground beside her, the winner from the last game was on a roll.

"Gonna make it two in a row," she said to me, winking at Arnold.

"Not if I can help it," Arnold said, winking back at me.

"Best prizes on the boardwalk," Betty called out, desperate for a few more players.

"China vases, chess sets, teapots, silverware. I've got it. All you have to do is win!"

A middle-aged man in Bermuda shorts and a plaid shirt was sucked in.

"I need a new teapot," he said, handing Betty a quarter.

Two teenage girls joined us. They were eyeing the stuffed animals on the top rack.

"Imagine how much fun it would be to sleep with him," one of them said, pointing to the tiger at the end of the row.

Betty rang the warning buzzer. "Ten seconds to race time," she said, beginning her count-down. I began to scratch my right shoulder. I don't know why but whenever I get nervous my shoulder itches or my right leg, or when I'm really nervous, my whole back.

Five. Four. Three. Two. One. The bell rang. I slammed my hand onto the lever and began to hit it as hard and as fast as I could. From the corner of my eye, I could see two other dogs in front of me.

The itch was getting worse. I tried to get my mind off of it. I thought about the prize I would choose if I won. Stuffed animals collected dust and we were forbidden to have them in our rooms. The teapot was pretty but I was sure that Mrs. H would confiscate it. What I really wanted was something for Beverly, a prize that would make her love me.

I kept slamming the handle, over and over again. I was thinking about life in the orphanage and about how much I wanted to get out of there.

The bell rang and Betty screamed, "It's number 11. Eleven's the winner"

I jumped up and down and whistled as loudly as I could.

Arnold grinned. He was glad that I had beaten him.

"What do you want?" Betty asked, pointing to the prizes. I hesitated for a moment, drawn to the chess set. I had always wanted one. Arnold was teaching me to play.

I knew how to set up the board and which pawn to lead with. It was a beautiful set with inlaid checkerboard squares and intricately carved pieces.

"Give me the goldfish," I said pointing to the bowl that was sitting on the second shelf. There were two fish swimming in it—round and round they chased one another, through a yellow tunnel and a blue castle.

"Beverly will love the goldfish," I said to Arnold before he could say a word.

We walked home slowly. I held the fishbowl with both hands so that the water did not spill.

Dinner was almost ready when we arrived and Beverly was busy in the kitchen. I decided to hide the goldfish and surprise her with the gift when we were eating dessert. I put the bowl in the closet in the hall and sat down on the living room sofa.

The kitchen door opened and Beverly appeared. She was wearing a flowered apron and she carried a plate of hot fish sticks.

"Dip them in the tartar sauce," Beverly said, point to the creamy white sauce in the middle of the platter.

I hated fish sticks, really I did. Mrs. H served them twice a week and we were forced to eat two. But I knew better than to refuse.

"My favorites," I said, reaching for one and dipping it quickly.

Arnold smacked his lips. He was already downing his third one.

Beverly watched as I chewed.

I nearly gasped when she announced that we each could eat four. Beverly always did that, counting out food, the way she counted coins. The fish sticks were dry and tasteless and the tartar sauce did not help at all. I gritted my teeth and finished my portion.

Beverly picked up the empty plate. "Dinner's ready," she said, shooing us into the kitchen.

We sat down and waited as Beverly took two pot holders and removed the casserole from the oven. She placed the round Pyrex covered dish on a trivet in the center of the table. A brown sauce bubbled ferociously.

"It's the spec-ial-ty of la maison," Beverly laughed, "my famous chicken, mushrooms and artichoke hearts casserole, simmered in soy sauce and sherry."

I hated mushrooms even more than I hated fish sticks and I hated artichoke hearts even more than mushrooms. That left only the chicken.

Beverly placed a mound of white rice on Arnold's plate and spooned three tablespoons of the chicken casserole over it.

"I'm giving you a double helping," she said, doling out six tablespoons to me. "You're a growing boy!"

In a moment she returned with a second casserole. "It's my spinach souffle," she said. "You'll love it."

Arnold joked about Popeye the Sailor Man and how good spinach was for me.

"Make a muscle, Joey," he said. "Show Beverly how strong you are."

I flexed my right arm and held my breath.

Beverly leaned over and squeezed my forearm. "Hard as a rock," she said, winking at Arnold.

The casserole was very salty and I drank three glasses of water. The spinach souffle had no taste at all. I felt as if I was chewing paper.

"Save room for dessert," Beverly said after we had all nearly finished our plates.

She cleared the table and brought out a large chocolate cake.

"Happy anniversary!" Beverly said to Arnold. He leaned over and kissed her. They had met exactly two years ago.

I stood up and walked into the living room. I took the fishbowl out of the closet and carried it carefully into the kitchen, stopping in front of Beverly.

"It's for you," I said. "I won it at the greyhound arcade." I moved the bowl toward Beverly, expecting her to take it from me but she sat there frozen in her seat.

Her face had a pained look and her mouth seemed to be twitching.

"Goldfish," she said, her voice cracking. She was running her fingers through her hair nervously.

"Two of them," I said, proud of my gift.

Beverly was silent. I put the fishbowl down in the center of the table, next to the half-eaten chicken casserole.

"Goldfish grow very fast," Arnold said, trying to start the conversation. "You have to be careful not to feed them too much."

"We had goldfish at the orphanage," I said. "Tiny and Big. One was a runt and the other was a giant."

Arnold laughed. "Good names," he said.

Beverly did not think it funny. "Fish don't live very long," she said, finally breaking her silence. "When I was eight years old, my mother bought me two for my birthday. I fed them every day and I changed the water when it was dirty. I remember the smell." Beverly sighed. "They lived with me for three months."

"What happened?" Arnold asked.

"I woke up one morning and went to feed the fish and they were floating dead in the bowl. One of my father's friends had doused his cigar in there the night before at their poker game. I cried and cried. My mother said that it was ridiculous to cry over fish and even more ridiculous to bury them. She flushed their poor dead bodies down the toilet."

I felt sick. Beverly was staring at Arnold. The fish in the bowl were staring at me.

Poor kid, they seemed to be saying to me with their fishy gaze, can't you do anything right?

The fish were chasing each other, darting through the green plants. Round and round, they swam, churning the water as they circled. Dinner was over. I stood up to clear the plates. Beverly removed the unfinished casserole. Arnold picked up the silverware and the glasses. Only the fishbowl remained in the center of the kitchen table.

I knew what I had to do. "The kids will love them at the orphanage," I said, picking up the fishbowl and hugging it tightly against my chest.

Dog Tags

Fall 1958

MY DOG TAG WEIGHED almost nothing. Made of tin, it hung on a beaded chain. Embossed letters announced my name, my address, and my religion. When the atomic bomb landed, they would know who I was and where to bury me. That was what my teacher told the class on a Wednesday morning. My tag listed the address of the orphanage and my assigned religion: Roman Catholic.

For all I knew, I was Episcopalian or Jewish. There were Jews who had grey eyes like mine. I saw them walking back and forth on the boardwalk. Striking grey eyes shielded by dark eyebrows. If it were up to me, that's what I would be: Jewish. Like Beverly and Arnold.

Jews were smarter than other people. In my 12 years, I had already learned that fact. They could figure out what you were going to do before you did it and trick you, too, if you weren't paying attention. Four slices of rye bread could cost a nickel or a dime—depending on how many fingers leaned on the scale. You could buy two sour pickles for a nickel or four for fifteen cents, if you weren't careful.

I watched Beverly at the skeeball arcade, her magical fingers dispensing nickels to the players. She'd reach into the register and scoop out a handful of nickels. "Usually, I get it on the nose," Beverly told me. "One dollar's worth of nickels. I can tell by the weight. Here, try to do it." I leaned over and grabbed a handful of nickels, then began to count them.

"You've only got 16," Beverly said. "I can see that already. But that was a good try." Beverly was sweet to console me. Yes, Jews were smarter, especially the boardwalk Jews who ran the arcades and the rides.

I sat in class watching my teacher's back. Miss Twining's flowered dress swayed as she wrote on the blackboard, swirls of pink and purple petunias dancing in the chalk dust. Her handwriting was round and even.

"What to do in case of an atomic bomb attack," she wrote in her perfect letters, turning to ask the class a question. "What would you do if there was an atom bomb warning?" she asked me. There was no avoiding her penetrating eyes. Framed by wire eyeglasses, they stared at me, waiting for my reply.

"I'd hide under my bed," I said, trying to give her a serious answer. That was a pretty safe thing to do, wasn't it? I'd hidden under there plenty of times when I was in trouble for not cleaning up my room or for forgetting to do the laundry. If you lay very still, your body rolled against the wall, it was a cool and comforting spot, especially when the floral quilt draped over the mattress, protecting you from prying eyes.

Mrs. Twining winced as I spoke. She didn't like my answer. "Hiding under your bed won't save you," she said, turning to Sally for a better response. Sally was busy doodling in her notebook and she didn't look up at first. Then, feeling the heat of Mrs. Twining's gaze, she put her pencil down and tilted her chin in the teacher's direction.

"I'd hide in the bomb shelter," Sally said, making a "this-is-the-answer-she-wanted" face at me. Sally was always trying to make me feel bad. We both lived at the orphanage, but she was Miss Goodie Two-Shoes, the little girl Mrs. Hutchinson would have had if she had ever married, which she hadn't.

I couldn't imagine anyone wanting to marry her. She was just too mean. At least, she was too mean to me. She'd always find a spot on one of the dishes I washed or a speck of dust on the top of the bookcase in the library, after it was my turn to clean it. Nothing I did pleased her.

"Joey, can't you get anything right?" she would say at least a hundred times a day. Her voice changed completely when she talked to Sally. "Beautiful job," she said, touring the kitchen after Sally cleaned up. "Couldn't have done it better myself."

Mrs. Twining must have conferred with Mrs. Hutchinson because she treated Sally the same way. "The bomb shelter," she said, "now that's the right answer. Do we all remember what a bomb shelter is?" Everyone's hand went up, except mine. I wasn't even going to try.

Once a month, we held practice drills. There was a warning siren from the fire station in the middle of town. A loud wail announced "Be on the alert." We kids marched single file down the stairs into the basement, where we put on helmets and crouched on the floor. The shelter was cold and damp. I fingered my dog tag, feeling the raised letters like a blind person. There was a sharp spot at the top of the capital letter J which always snagged my T-shirt. Another rough spot on the G for Gibbons.

I was third on the line, behind Bobby and, unfortunately, in front of Billy—who could be counted on to cause trouble. He poked me in the back twice. "Watch your step," he said. "If you don't, a rat might bite you." He snickered and closed his mouth so that I could hear his top molars bang into his bottom ones. A few seconds later, he pinched my hand hard. "Did you hear what I said?" he asked. I nodded my head and inched away from him.

Mrs. Twining gave us our instructions. "Don't talk. Don't whisper. No giggling," she said. "Wait for the all-clear siren—two long wails—before you stand up. Anyone who fools around will end up in detention." The threat of detention hung over our heads. One false move and you'd be forced to stay after school writing "I promise to behave during a bomb shelter drill" 2,000 times before Mrs. Twining would release you. The torture could go on for two weeks.

We discussed The Bomb often. The Russians had one. And they would blow us all up—if we didn't get them first—that's what we kids thought. We all had our plans, just in case we had to evacuate. I had a shoebox ready to go. Inside were my two best shooter marbles, a red flashlight and four extra batteries, a small canteen, two chocolate bars, a pack of Juicy Fruit gum, a deck of cards, a pocket knife, a ball of string, a notepad, two pencils and five dollars. Sally inspected my box and laughed. "That stuff won't save you," she said. Her shoebox contained two pairs of white socks, a pink lipstick, a mirror, and a box of animal crackers. She promised to share the cookies with me—if I shared my chocolate bars.

On a Friday morning in June the siren began to wail before we left for school. I was eating breakfast in the cafeteria when it started ringing, vibrating the cereal spoon in my bowl. Mrs. Hutchinson appeared within seconds, clutching the air raid manual. She herded us kids into the hall, and then marched us all down the stairs into the basement storage room. I could hear her whispering to the cook, Ed Smith, who was still wearing his white apron, his fingers covered with pancake batter.

"We didn't have this on our schedule," she said, loud enough for me to hear. I squeezed Sally's hand. This was the first time that we had not been told about the drill the evening before. "This time it's for real," Sally said, "and my shoebox won't do me any good. It's upstairs."

I let go of her hand and moved to the back of the group. The basement was dark and the siren was still wailing. I slipped out the back door, ran around the corner and jumped the steps to the front porch, three at a time. Then, I headed upstairs, stopping in Sally's room to grab her shoebox from under her bed and moving on to my room, where my treasures were hidden behind the radiator cover. With both boxes under my arm, I returned to the shelter, through the entrance by the garbage pickup.

Ed Smith was shining a flashlight on the manual and Mrs. Hutchinson was reading from section 3, paragraph 8—the subject was gas masks. Ed shone the light on the green mask that Mrs. Hutchinson was waving in the air. "First you put the back flap over your head," she said. "Then you position the mouthpiece over your lips and turn the knob to the left to activate the air supply." While the children watched, she placed the mask on her face.

Two of the older boys began to laugh. She sure looked ridiculous.

Mrs. Hutchinson removed the mask and walked over to one of them. She pinched his cheek hard and then, as if that wasn't enough, smacked his face.

"Nothing funny is going on here," she said. "You're in big trouble."

Sally and I sat next to each other, our arms around our shoeboxes. According to Mrs. Hutchinson, by the time we counted to 200, the sirens would stop wailing and the drill would be over. I began to count softly.

Sally joined in. By the time we reached 99, we were beginning to feel scared.

"What if it isn't a drill?" she said, in between 99 and 100. "The bomb might be minutes away." Sally was beginning to hyperventilate.

The basement door opened a crack and two men came down the stairs. One of them whispered something to Mrs. Hutchinson who nodded. She looked serious—the way she looked when she was about to pinch your ear or whack your knuckles with a ruler.

Sally had stopping counting now. I was up to 139 and I was having trouble remembered what number I was up to.

"Bomb scares aren't for real," I said. "They're just like going to the movies. The only things we're missing is the buttered popcorn." Of course, I didn't believe a word of what I was telling her. But there are times when lying is the only right response. Telling the truth just causes too much pain.

Mrs. Hutchinson was listening to a small radio. From where I was sitting I could only hear the sound of the voices—not their words.

"What are they saying?" Sally asked. "Is this real or fake?"

Mrs. Hutchinson did not answer. She was still hunched over her small radio, listening intently.

After a few seconds, she removed the radio from her ear and announced. "The Chief of Security is about to speak. I'll know more soon."

"See," Sally said, poking me hard. "I told you this was no dress rehearsal. We're going to be bombed to smithereens."

For a moment, I could see Sally blowing apart into pieces, her long brown braids twisting and turning in the sky like a tornado. I was flying by her side—or at least some part of me was—talking to her. I was looking down through the clouds, trying to make out the green roof of the orphanage.

"We're on alert," Mrs. Hutchinson said, bringing me back to earth. "They've sighted a Russian jet flying towards New York City. Washington and Moscow are in negotiations but we have to take the threat seriously."

I was fingering my dog tag as she spoke. I didn't want to end up in heaven with the nuns and the priests. I'd rather be with Beverly and Arnold, playing poker and drinking beer. Nobody could fool them. Forget about this paradise stuff. This Garden of Eden circling above.

The boy in front of me began to squirm. It was Philip Goldberg, a fat kid who was the best student in life sciences class but who couldn't hit a baseball. Philip turned his head and looked at me. He was crying.

"No more homemade chocolate chip cookies," he said. "No more pizza with extra cheese and pepperoni. We'll all starve and die. Just because of those Commies. You can't trust a Russian."

I reached over and patted Philip on the shoulder. Philip was plenty smart but he was definitely a coward. It was too early to cave in. Too early to concede. I wanted to console him. I really did. But consolation was worth something. You didn't just give it away. Life in the orphanage had taught me that. Life was about trading this for that. The smartest kid got the best trade. A brand new Spalding for a whistle that didn't blow. A Yankees baseball cap for a dirty book—where the best pages were cut out.

I was the master trader, renowned for my persuasive skills. Philip could use one of my chocolate bars right now. But what, if anything, did he have to give me in return? Sitting there in the dark, sweating in his oversize T-shirt. We were about to be goners anyway so why did the deal matter?

I couldn't answer that question. A deal is a deal. Doesn't matter if you are about to be blown to pieces. You still have to outwit your opponent. Get more than you give. That's the code. You can't break it. Part of me just wanted to give Philip the candy bar and stop his whining. The other part was hard at work trying to come up with a trade.

I was fingering my cold dog tag when the idea came to me. Philip and I would exchange dog tags. He would become Joe Gibbons and I would become Philip Goldberg. In one deft switch, I would become a Jew, ensuring my fate. There was no way that the nuns and the priests could get me then. I'd live with Beverly and Arnold and their cronies. We would spend our days playing pinochle and telling dirty jokes. I would run the hot-dog concession.

I reached into my shoebox and pulled out a chocolate bar. Then, I inched close to Philip and whispered in his ear. "I've got just what you need," I said, waiving the large Hershey bar under his nose.

His nostrils twitched, acknowledging the sweet aroma of chocolate.

"You can have the whole thing," I said, "if we can make a little trade."

"What sort of trade?" Philip asked. He was leaning forward, breathing in the smell of the chocolate.

"Our dog tags," I said. "You'll wear mine and I'll wear yours."

"Because I've always admired you. You're the smartest kid in our class. I'll never be able to think like you but wearing your dog tag I can pretend, can't I?"

I wasn't sure that Philip would buy the flattery. But he surprised me.

"You've always admired me?" he said. "Amazing!" He removed his dog tag from around his neck and handed it to me. I handed him mine. Then, sort of ceremoniously, I placed the Hershey bar in his waiting hands.

In the dark, I could hear Philip tearing through the wrapper. I could hear his teeth chomping on the chocolate. I sat on the floor fingering my new identity: Philip Goldberg. Age 12. Religion: Jewish.

The Wrong Side of Town

Summer 1959

THE WEST END. Where the boardwalk stopped, where the land narrowed and the houses shrunk. Sandy streets lined with wood-framed houses, bungalows, set side by side—1500 feet separating the ocean from the bay.

No one with money lived in this side of town. The rich people clustered in the East End; the middle class were spread out in the center of town; and the blue-collar workers, mostly Irish Catholic, lived in the West End, where you could hear every word of your neighbor's fight with her husband, even when she whispered.

The orphanage stood on the last good block, before the tangle of bungalows. Looking west from the assembly room on the third floor, I could see the West End, its flimsy buildings hugging the sand. Many of the boys I played stickball with lived there in rooms that smelled of mildew. After school, I'd often walk to the empty lot by the bay that we appropriated as our private playing field. At low tide, the smell was terrible from washed-up garbage, sewage, dead fish wrapped in seaweed, and rotting crab bodies. When we took a break, we sat on the bulkhead, watching the water splash the wall and the horseshoe crabs hump each other.

"Just like my parents," Brian Conklin told me one day as we studied the action. Brian claimed to have done it, although I wasn't sure I believed him. He said that he had screwed Kathleen under the boardwalk when he was 13. Now that he was 14, he told us endless stories about his conquests. Most of us were virgins and we envied Brian.

"My parents don't even close their bedroom door," Brian said, never taking his eyes off the crabs. Brian's father was a sanitation man. He looked like Charles Atlas, the bodybuilder whose ad ran on the inside back cover of the Superman comics. Charles Atlas's chest was a perfect triangle—muscular broad shoulders tapering down to a narrow waist. If I had a dollar to spare, which I didn't, I would have mailed in the coupon for his exercise pamphlet—the one that promised to reveal all of his secrets.

Brian's mother wore bright pink lipstick which matched the polish on her fingers and toes. Her hair was dyed blonde and a cigarette was always dangling from her lips. She worked as a cashier in the drug store four mornings a week. That left plenty of time for afternoons playing canasta with her cronies or swimming at the beach. Only Brian and his younger sister, Patricia, were still living at home. The others—Keith, Paul, Dennis, and Mary, had all moved out. Maybe fled. Keith and Paul had joined the army. Dennis was working as a mechanic near Miami and Mary had married Bill, who worked for the phone company.

They were the quintessential West End family—good Catholics with six hard-working kids who would punch you in the nose if you crossed them. On Halloween, they'd squirt you with seltzer—to test your mettle. The loot was definitely better trick-or-treating in the East End but the West End was much more of an adventure. You could get hurt there. Mrs. Hutchinson knew that and she banned us from heading west. We defied her orders. Brian was our protector. We trusted him to lead us from house to house, ringing the doorbell first.

"Stand behind me," he said. "And, remember, no wise guy stuff." Brian would ring the bell three or four times, and then knock on the door. "Anybody alive in there?" he'd yell. That was the drill—not some timid ring, followed by a meek, "Trick or Treat." No, you had to be prepared to retaliate—if you were rejected. And Brian was. He had his sack of flour to decorate the doors of the folks who were too cheap to cough up loot.

I wasn't a member of Brian's gang. I was too timid for that. Hanging out at Playworld with Arnold or at the skeeball arcade with Beverly was more my speed. But occasionally, when I was feeling brave, I'd walk down to the sandlot by the bay and join the game. I played third base and I was pretty good at it, so they were always glad to see me.

These were tough kids whose fathers drank too many beers at The Shamrock after work, perched on tall wooden stools, avoiding going home. Why would they want to go home anyway? Home was crowded, a beat-up bungalow with six or seven kids vying for attention and no place to hide. Home was a tired, bitter wife in a flowered housedress who started yelling the minute you walked in the door.

Life at the orphanage was bad, but life in the West End was worse. Hard to believe, but to me it was meaner, tougher, and less predictable. I knew that I would get whipped if I didn't put my light out or thrashed if I hid food in my room. But I was spared a vicious pummeling by a drunken dad who couldn't remember what he had done the next morning—especially not the right punch he had thrown in his son's eye. I was lucky, sort of. Lucky, if you understood luck in a perverse way and I did. I had to.

We sat side by side, studying the humping horseshoe crabs, and staring into the water.

"The shipment's coming in tonight," Brian said, assuming that I understood what he meant. "John is bringing it from Chinatown in his brother's car. We're meeting here at ten."

I didn't say a word. That wouldn't be cool. So I just nodded, encouraging him to continue speaking.

"This year we've got three-stage rockets," he said. He emphasized the three-stage part, to impress me with his technical expertise. I was your basic, light-it-and-run firecracker kid—three red crackers jammed in my pant's pocket, with a package of sparklers sticking out at the top.

Nothing was more sacrosanct than the Fourth, a day when the thugs of the West End lit up the night sky. Only on rare occasions did the police interfere. Most of the time, they hung around, watching the show, and cautioning the kids to be careful. "You could blow off a couple of fingers with one mistake," Officer Finnegan reminded me, holding up his broad hand that was missing his pinkie finger. I stared at the fat stub, snapped off just above the first joint.

There were years when the cops actually helped out, lighting the big rockets in metal drums. After all, they were kids themselves, Irish kids who had grown up on the tough streets of the West End. Now, they'd come back to work the neighborhood and patrol the boardwalk—Mrs. Delehanty's altar boy, carrying a night stick.

I knew that it was best not to mess with them. You couldn't afford to be fresh or they'd crack you across the face and threaten to tell the priest and your mother, if you had one, and I didn't.

I had seen the remains of the rockets, heavy charred curls of red and blue cardboard, lying in the sand. I was afraid to light one—worried that Brian would honor me by asking me to do so. Making me, the orphan, by this official rite, one of the gang. What would I do if he did that? Run away? Start to cry?

Actually hold the long match to the wick and watch it sizzle?

The thought made my fingers burn. Right before my eyes, blisters appeared and the skin turned red. I was afraid of fire. For good reason. Once, on a windy fall day, I saw a three-story wooden frame house in the West End burn to the ground in what seemed to be a few seconds. I stood on the street watching the wind—which was blowing from the ocean—whip the flames, higher and higher, redder and redder. By the time the fire department arrived, it was too late. They sprayed water on the building, eventually putting out the flames and reducing it to a pile of smoldering rubble. Outside, on the street, the O'Briens, the family who lived there, huddled together, their three-year-old screaming for his teddy bear.

"Dodo," he cried, "I want Dodo." He pounded his fist against his mother's cotton dress and would not be consoled.

I learned a big lesson that day. The safest thing to do was to avoid fire at all costs. And fire meant firecrackers, too. I could put on a big act and pretend to be brave but I wasn't. I was a coward. The trick was how to avoid showing it.

"You'll be my assistant this year," Brian said, patting me on the shoulder. "Jimmy's away and I know that I can trust you." He continued to pat my right shoulder. I could tell that he was waiting for my enthusiastic response. I thought of saying that Mrs. Hutchinson had banned our going to the fireworks, that she was going to lock the orphanage doors early to prevent us from drifting down to the beach for the display. But I didn't think that would convince Brian. He knew that I had snuck out before.

"Thanks for asking me," I said. "But I promised to help Arnold in Play-world. He asked me last night and I wouldn't want to disappoint him." I held my breath hoping that he would buy the excuse.

Brian laughed. "Arnold's a pushover. I'll ask him, if you don't want to. So, it's a yes." He reached over and grabbed my hand and shook it. "A deal's a deal," he said.

I didn't even try to protest. He was right. Arnold was a big softie—a guy who would say yes before he even thought of saying no. All the kids knew that. My alibi hadn't worked.

I shook Brian's hand, working hard to keep my own hand from trembling. I could already feel the trembling in my chest and it wouldn't be long before it reached my fingers.

"Arnold will understand," I said. There was no way that I could say what

Brian wanted to hear.

"Be here early," Brian said, "around 8:30. It will take us at least a half hour to set things up." All of a sudden, Brian laughed. Then, he snickered.

"I knew that guy would be the BIG winner," he said, pointing to the largest of the crabs who was now in prime position. "Crabs are just like people," he said. "Pushy, aggressive, clawing their way through the sand."

The thought of their competition made Brian sweat. He pursed his lips together in a tight grimace, imitating the crabs. I felt his pain, like the pinch of the crab's pincers in cold water. Ouch. Get out of my way. This is my world—not yours. Swim somewhere else.

A tanker went by, stirring up the water and causing waves to crash on the beach. For a moment, the crabs disengaged. Then, the big one lunged and was back on top.

"See you later," Brian said as he got up to leave.

I walked up Beech Street on my way to Playworld. I didn't really have to go there. Arnold was not expecting me to work. It had all been a lie—a lie that had failed. But I needed to see Arnold and talk to him. I needed to talk to someone about firecrackers and my fear of fire and my commission as Brian's assistant.

Arnold was standing by the entrance, with a hammer in one hand and a piece of two by four in the other. On the ground, in front of him, was a saw and bag of nails.

"You're just in time to help me," he called out as I approached. "The front post rotted out and I'm making a new one." I could tell that Arnold was happy to see me, not just because he needed my assistance. Arnold loved me. I was not just some poor orphan kid whom he had befriended.

I placed my hand on the post and waited for instructions.

"Put your fingers here," Arnold said as he pointed to a corner of the post. "And don't move. I don't want to miss the nail and hit your hand."

I did exactly as he said. He reached down to the bag and took out a long nail, placed it carefully on the top of the two by four and began to hammer—inches from my fingers. It was strange but I did not feel afraid. You could trust Arnold.

"Going to the fireworks at the bay tonight?" I asked him, when he paused to get another nail. "I'll be there shooting rockets." I wondered if he would disapprove.

"I love July 4th," Arnold said. "When I was a kid in Brooklyn, we'd sneak down to the beach and shoot off firecrackers." He winked at me when he said the word "sneak."

"Guess kids always sneak out," I said, averting my eyes. I still didn't know whether he was coming to the fireworks but I was not going to ask him again.

He was almost finished making the post now.

"Don't be scared," Arnold said as I started to leave. I hadn't said a word about being scared but I didn't have to. Arnold always knew what I was feeling.

"Being scared is a state of mind. You can talk yourself out of it." He patted me on the shoulder and smoothed my hair.

I ran all the way home. It was my turn to serve dinner and being late was a bad idea. Getting in trouble before fireworks would be the kiss of death. The smell of meatloaf greeted me as I entered the dining hall. There was a strong odor of onions and tomato sauce. I could see the plates lined up, thick brown slices slathered with sauce. I was to add the canned green beans to each plate and I was to serve them, too.

"Where have you been?" Frances asked as she handed me an apron. "Hutchinson's been on the warpath. I lied and told her that I'd just seen you and that you said you'd be down in a minute."

I slipped on the apron and began spooning beans onto the plates.

"Handling some July 4th business," I said, avoiding giving her a fuller explanation. There was no point doing that. The less she knew the better. Hutchinson wouldn't be able to squeeze it out of her—like the last bit of toothpaste from the tube.

I was thinking about Brian and the rockets. If I wasn't careful, I could lose a finger or two. For a moment, I imagined my hand maimed, bandaged. I was standing by the boardwalk begging, a tin cup in my good hand. Arnold dropped a quarter in the cup, shook his head and walked on.

The line was thinning. I filled a plate for myself and sat down at the end of one of the long tables. I wasn't hungry. Fireworks were on my brain. John sat down next to me.

"I hear that you're Brian's main man tonight," he said. Then, just to make sure that I understood his point, he said, "Don't screw up!"

All evening I obsessed on the screwing up part. I could see the headline in the local paper: "Orphan blows off three fingers in firecracker mishap." Below the headline, there would be a photo of me, hand bandaged, being led down the brick steps of the hospital by Mrs. Hutchinson. "It's hard to control these children," Mrs. Hutchinson told the reporter. "We do our best, but remember that without mothers and fathers they are easily tempted by the forces of evil."

I did not smile for the camera and I said nothing. Instead, I gazed straight ahead, my eyes focused on some far-off place. The story examined in great detail how wild West End boys with orphans in tow, blew their fingers off in an unsupervised fireworks display on the bay beach. Police Department Captain John Gillespie was quick to condemn the hooligans. "By the time we raided the beach, it was too late," Gillespie said. "Had our men in blue been there, this would not have happened."

I snickered as I imagined the story. Sure. That was what the captain would say. But the cops were down there helping. Wasn't Officer O'Hara the man who taught the boys how to light the wick with the long match?

I lay on my cot, worrying. I couldn't let Brian down or the whole West End would consider me a coward. But I was a coward. Sort of.

It was getting dark. I had promised to meet Brian at 8:30. Sneaking out was easy. I reached under my cot for the three pillows I had stashed there and arranged them under my army blanket. Nobody at the orphanage was better at this than me. I even had a head with a brown wig for the pillow.

I shut out the lights, slipped down the back stairs, and fled through the pantry door. It was a routine I knew well. Mrs. Hutchinson would be up in her room, drinking chamomile tea and reading The New York Times. She rarely came downstairs after 8:00 PM.

On the streets, there were signs that July 4th had already begun—burnt out sparklers lying in the gutters. I picked one up and twirled it as I headed toward the bay beach. Brian was waiting for me—skimming stones into the water. He had a way of making them travel to the middle of the bay before they gave in to gravity and sank.

I had given up on stone skimming having no aptitude whatsoever for the art. What did I have a talent for? Helping Arnold with the go carts at Playworld. Counting coins. Safe, easy tasks, yes, those were my specialties. No one could ever accuse me of being too bold.

"Right on time," I could hear Brian greeting me as I approached the beach. He was leaning into a large metal drum. Bobby and Michael stood behind him. "We have a half hour to set things up," Brian said, motioning for me to join him.

"Here, hold this," Brian continued, handing me a large rocket. My fingers trembled as I touched the red cardboard.

"Don't be afraid. It won't bite you," he said laughing.

My job was to organize the fireworks—grouping rockets with rockets and cherry bombs with cherry bombs. After all, Brian told me, this wasn't just about noise. It was art. There was a design, a beautiful design, to the evening's show. Brian was the consummate artist—arranging the spectacle to elicit gasps of approval from the crowd.

When I arrived only three kids were there. Ten minutes later thirty kids were gathered on the beach, scruffy West End kids with torn T-shirts and jeans.

"You're my main man tonight," Brian told me as we worked side by side. "You hold the rocket while I light it. Be steady and do what I tell you to do." He could see the fear in my eyes. "Don't mess up—or both of us will get hurt."

Messing up. I was great at messing up, especially when I was afraid. The crowd was building. There were now close to 100 kids on the beach—with a sprinkling of curious grownups. Still, no cops were on the scene although Brian assured me that one or two of them would show up eventually.

"We'll start at 9:30," Brian said. According to my watch, which was always five minutes slow, that gave us 12 more minutes. Someone was waving to me from the crowd—it was Arnold in a white shirt and a red baseball cap. Next to him stood Beverly—wrapped in a bright blue shawl. Together, they were the American flag. I waved back at him and smiled. It didn't surprise me that Arnold had come down to the beach for the fireworks. After all, a man whose life was devoted to making go-carts fly by just had to be a kid at heart.

The kids began to clap their hands and stomp their feet. They were tired of waiting.

"Count down from a hundred," Brian yelled at them. Before he finished the words, they were at 97.

"That'll hold them off for just about the right amount of time," he said, handing me the box of matches. He emphasized the word right, looking up at me to be sure that I understood.

My right fingers were trembling and my right eye began to twitch. I could count on that eye to misbehave whenever I was nervous. Ring. Like an alarm clock, it went off.

"Don't let me down or you'll regret it for the rest of your life," Brian said.

I looked up and tried to make eye contact with Arnold, who had just arrived. Maybe he would save me. Maybe Arnold would jump up, grab the match from my hand and light the rocket. But Arnold's face was turned sideways. He was talking to Beverly and they were laughing. I couldn't see one thing to laugh about.

Suddenly, Arnold stopped laughing. He turned and stared at me. At my face. At my trembling hands. Then, he mumbled something to Beverly and began to run through the crowd, pushing two kids out of his way as he shoved forward.

"Gotta let old Arnold in on the fun," he yelled as he neared Brian and me. "It's not right that you kids monopolize everything on July 4th."

Arnold took the match from my hand and waved it in the air. Then, he turned to Brian and asked, "Are you ready?"

Brian was stunned. But he recovered quickly. The crowd was waiting.

"Now," Brian said as Arnold hit the long match against the striker and lit the fuse.

With his powerful right arm, Brian threw the rocket up into the air. Then the three of us backed up to join the crowd. The rocket sailed upward in the dark sky, exploding over the bay. All that was left were concentric circles of cascading white lights, lingering beneath the stars.

Jollie Trixie Keeps from Getting Blue

1960

"CALL ME JOLLY TRIXIE," she said, as she extended her hand. "My real name is Blanche," she whispered. "But I much prefer Jolly Trixie." I reached for her fat fingers and pressed them against my own. Her hand was hot and sweaty and her skin very soft. She had been selling hot dogs from a white wooden cart just outside the skeeball arcade for nearly two weeks.

Her thick arms dug into the cauldron of sauerkraut, and she smeared bright yellow mustard with a wooden stick across each frankfurter. She mopped her brow with a large red handkerchief. I thought about inviting her inside to cool off.

"What a name!" I said, trying hard not to stare at the dark circles under her eyes. "Where did you ever find it?"

"In a book about the boardwalk," she said. "Jolly Trixie was a Coney Island sideshow dancer who weighed 685 lbs and stood 5 feet 4 inches. She performed the hootchy kootchy under a big silver banner that read, 'She's so fat that it takes seven men to hug her.'"

She spread her arms sideways as far as she could.

"That fat!" she said. "I'm only half her weight, so it would only take three and one-half men to hug me."

I could see that she expected me to laugh but I couldn't. The best thing I could do was to give her a half smile. "I'm Beverly," I said, "Beverly Bridges. Real name's Norma Beverly Bluestein. And, I'm so skinny that half a man could hug me or at the very least three-quarters of one." The last time I jumped on one of the "Guess Your Weight" scales in the penny arcade, I barely hit 100 pounds.

Arnold would have been insulted by my quip. I could just hear him protesting that he was not half a man or three-quarters of one. I could see him flexing his right bicep to prove his point. Still, the fact was that together we weighed less than Jolly Trixie. What a thought!

I winked at her and she winked back, a sure sign that we had become friends. That's the way it is on the boardwalk. One minute you and the person sitting next to you on the green wooden bench were strangers, staring straight ahead at the waves crashing on the beach, and the next you're telling them about how you were mistreated by your mother when you were five and locked yourself in the pink bathroom for five hours.

I remembered telling absolute strangers stories about my father, Marvin (real name Menachem), who was the shop steward in a dress factory and who got caught bringing home a sample to my mother—almost lost his job for it. And about my mother, Shirley, who woke up one morning, decided that she needed a lift, and dyed her dark brown hair ash blonde. When my father came home from work, he didn't like what he saw. He cursed at her in Yiddish, "Zoyne!" he said. "Whore." He slapped her hard across the face, right in front of me. The next day her brown hair had returned. We never spoke about the incident. You buried stuff. That was the way things were in my family.

Not on the boardwalk, though. Everything surfaced. The potency of the sea air pulled secrets from your soul. Tiny secrets, big secrets, they all escaped, sucked out by the undertow. Or beached by the incoming tide, stranded on the sand, like seaweed.

I was sure that Jolly Trixie had hundreds of secrets—one for every wrinkle, for every fold of her skin. There was a sad look in her eyes, large brown eyes framed by bright blue eye shadow and black mascara. Life isn't easy, they said. Trouble lurks around the corner. Laugh as much as you can, whenever you can. Otherwise, you'll be crying.

I bought a hot dog and invited her in to play a few games, handing her a fistful of nickels, which she promptly dumped into her jacket pocket. She surprised me by rolling the ball up the alley right into the center hole. 50 points. Definitely not a beginner.

"I've played before," Jolly Trixie said, "lots of times—in Atlantic City and in Coney Island." She knew how to throw a curve ball, all right. Her second ball landed in the 40-point circle—just missing the center by a hair.

"Some of us just spend our whole lives on boardwalks," she said, "we're addicted." She laughed a loud laugh, then reached for another coin.

I was addicted too—I knew that—to little bags of salted peanuts and to the tangy yellow mustard that streaked the burnt skin of my hot dog. When I ate out in civilized restaurants, the food was bland. I would reach for the salt shaker before lifting my fork to my mouth. Arnold would wink as I sprinkled salt over my plate.

"It's definitely not the boardwalk," he said. We had a weakness for food that left large grease spots on paper plates.

"Do you know my friend Arnold?" I asked her. "He runs Playworld."

"Can't say I've met him," she said, "But I'd like to. I love amusement parks. I've never been up in one of those swinging Ferris wheel cages, though. There's just no way that I could squeeze into one of them, especially not at the Kiddie Rides. But I love the way the cages fly through space." She raised her heavy arms and flapped them in the air, pretending to soar.

It was a graceful swoop, one you'd hardly expect from a woman who weighed 350 pounds. I bet she could dance, too, the rolls around her waist rippling as she moved. A fierce Lindy or a smoky foxtrot, with the right man of course. Not Arnold. He'd never be able to handle Jolly Trixie.

"I'm sure he'd like to meet you," I said, although I wasn't sure. Arnold was a fitness nut, lifting weights twice a day when he saw the slightest sign of flab. "We could have a late dinner together after we close down for the night, if that's not too late for you." I thought about what I would feed her. She looked like she could devour a bowl of spaghetti, probably a whole pound, with sauce—for a first course.

As if reading my thoughts, Jolly Trixie had a suggestion. You could tell, food was always on her mind. "I love pizza," she said. "The pepperoni at Pete's." As she spoke, she rolled her tongue around her lips, making a full, slow circle, salivating at the thought of a pie loaded with slices of greasy pepperoni. Arnold hated the stuff. He was sure that they dyed it red. Arnold insisted that pepperoni was really grey, the color of mold.

Trixie began rolling her cart toward the frozen custard stand. "Business is better over there," she said.

I began breaking rolls of nickels. The red paper was strong. You needed to whack it against the side of the cash register to make a slit in it. Then, like breaking an egg and separating the white from the yellow, I opened the crack slowly, pouring all of the nickels into the right compartment. Not a one landed on the floor.

My head ached and I longed for a nap. I had barely slept the previous night, having woken up at 3:30 in the morning. In the dark, I thought about Joey. He was mopping the linoleum floor of the arcade, his tin pail filled with soapy water. Joey was pushing the stick of the mop back and forth, leaning on it with his skinny body. He was on his third rinse and he kept asking me if I liked it. "Tell me when it's clean enough," he said.

Joey was an orphan who wanted a home and Arnold definitely wanted to give him one. There was no way that I could stop Arnold from taking Joey in. They had a bond—and it made me jealous. I should have been enough for Arnold. More than enough. Bold. Brash. Sexy. Mistress of the skeeball arcade. Queen of the Boardwalk. Why would Arnold need more than me? I could not think of one good reason for Arnold wanting Joey. We had talked about babies, one morning after the two of us lay side by side, drenched in sweat and stained with semen. Neither of us, we agreed, had time for babies.

But Arnold had time for Joey. He brought him to the arcade every week to teach him how to throw curve balls up the alley. The trick was in a sneaky little twist of the wrist that made the ball turn just before it landed in the center hole. Joey had finally mastered it, landing the ball in the 50-pointer. "You're the best, Arnold," he said, reaching over to give Arnold a big hug.

When he hugged him, I hurt. I had no room for Joey in my heart. Or for anyone else.

Just before ten in the evening, after pulling the metal gate over the skeeball arcade and padlocking it shut, I walked over to Playworld. Arnold was covering the last whip car with its red oilcloth jacket. He waved as I approached the entrance. I could see Jolly Trixie coming down the ramp from the boardwalk. She was wearing a hot pink hat and had a green polka dotted scarf tied around her neck. You couldn't miss her. She smiled at me and tipped her hat.

Arnold was in for a big surprise. I hadn't said a word about our menage a trois. He had caught Trixie's wave and I noticed a puzzled look on his face. Who was this pink and green lady who weighed more than the two of us combined? Arnold had a problem with fat. He was always pinching his stomach, to check if it was getting soft. Arnold could do 30 sit-ups without losing his breath, 28 more than I could do.

Trixie was carrying a large green shopping bag which was swinging from her shoulder.

I greeted her and we walked toward Arnold who stood waiting.

"Here's my new friend, Jolly Trixie," I said. "You've probably seen her selling hot dogs in front of the skeeball arcade. I've invited her to join us for pizza."

Trixie reached into her bag and pulled out a handful of chewy caramels which she placed in Arnold's outstretched hand.

"They're delicious," she said. "You never go wrong if you have a few in your pocket."

Arnold never ate candy but he took the caramels anyway. "Happy to meet you, Trixie," he said. "Any friend of Beverly is a friend of mine." The words came out with a stiff sound, although I didn't think that Trixie noticed.

We walked up Beech Street toward Pete's—Arnold and Trixie leading the way. They were already deep in a conversation about business. Arnold was giving Trixie his usual spiel on the decline in Playworld attendance and Trixie was giving him her account of hot dog sales–which were, according to her, flourishing.

"I'm selling over 100 franks a day," she said. "And there's a reason for it. The secret's in my sauerkraut. I make it myself. None of that canned stuff, that stinks of vinegar." She rubbed her nose as she spoke, as if to rid herself of the smell.

"Glad one of us is prospering," Arnold said, turning to glance at me. His look said: What a naive soul she is. How little she knows about the world. Can you imagine believing that the secret to success lay in sauerkraut. "Best sauerkraut I ever ate was at Coney Island," Arnold said, clearly humoring Trixie. "At Moishe's hotdog stand near the Steeplechase. Do you know the one I mean?"

"Moishe had three kinds of mustard," Trixie said. "The best was the brown spicy kind. He would never tell me where he got it. Since I've had my own stand, I've tasted every mustard I could buy, but I've never found it."

Arnold was impressed. I could tell by the way he was looking at Trixie. Here was a lady who knew her mustard.

We were half a block away from Pete's. If you took a deep breath, you could smell the pizza dough baking in the oven. Trixie was close to skipping—a strange, graceful elephant dancing in the center ring of the sidewalk. She was starving, she told Arnold. Hadn't eaten a thing since lunch—which consisted of four hotdogs loaded with sauerkraut, pickles, and mustard.

"I usually eat six," she boasted. "But I was so busy today that I barely could squeeze in four. If I keep this up, I'll lose more weight—which would make me sad. To be famous, you need to weigh close to five hundred pounds. I've been slipping lately—down to 320—lost ten pounds over the last two months." She sighed, and I could tell that, from the look on her face, she was serious.

"If you're fat, you have to be VERY FAT," Trixie continued, "or else you won't attract the crowds. The first Jolly Trixie was known all over the world. There were even pictures of her in French and German newspapers. Trixie dancing under the stage lights, her arms and legs like the stumps of a 100-year-old oak tree. Look at me," she said, "I'm barely fat."

Arnold and I were looking at her and she did look VERY FAT to us. At least, she looked FAT to me. I opened the door to Pete's and waited for Trixie to walk through. She just made it—there was a half-inch of space, at most, between her and the door jamb. And, without hesitation, she walked toward the table that stood in the middle of the restaurant, between the booths and the counter. Pete saw her coming and, after poking around in a back closet, he came out carrying a wooden chair—an old fashioned folding chair that was three times the size of the slatted seat that I sat on all day at the skeeball arcade. Peter set the chair up at the head of the table and waited for Trixie to sit down.

"Three pizzas," she said, "with extra pepperoni." She hesitated for a minute and turned to me. For a moment, I thought she was going to ask us for our order. "Do you like pepperoni?" she asked.

"Not really," I said, looking at Arnold for help. "But we can always pull the slices off if we don't want to eat them," Arnold said, smiling warmly at Trixie.

"And put on extra cheese," Trixie added. "Smother it with cheese." She reached down for a napkin to catch the drool that was dripping from her lips. "All my life, I've loved pizza," Trixie continued. "Hot or cold. For breakfast or in the middle of the night."

"Me, too," Arnold said, whispering the words as if in a confessional.

"Where did you grow up?" Arnold asked her. He was squinting in her direction, a sure sign that she had him. I reached over and touched his shoulder to distract him but he barely noticed.

"In Brooklyn," she said. "In a red-brick two-family attached house in Bensonhurst. My father, Ralph, was a tailor. He worked in a shop on Orchard Street. My mother sewed blouses piecemeal at home on an old industrial sewing machine that was installed in the front parlor, where the light was best. I was one of four children, the only girl. The youngest and the biggest. Even when I was little, I was big. My brothers were tall and skinny like my dad. Even my mother—who was short—was only a little overweight. But I was big from the beginning. Over ten pounds at birth. Nearly 30 pounds at one year. Everywhere you went in the neighborhood, you could hear people talking about what I ate. 'Blanche was here yesterday and she ate four peanut butter sandwiches.' Or 'Blanche ate so many pancakes, I used up a whole bottle of maple syrup.'"

Blanche, I mean Jolly Trixie, laughed, as she told her story. But it made me feel sad. The thought of a child that fat was not a laughing matter. I couldn't imagine that Blanche had found it funny, either. The other kids were probably miserable to her. Somehow, she had just smothered her feelings by devouring another jelly doughnut or by polishing off two chocolate fudge ice cream sundaes.

Pete arrived with the first pizza. It was covered with pepperoni—at least 15 pieces on each slice. I removed the pepperoni from two slices and placed one on Arnold's plate and the other on mine. Jolly Trixie took a knife and worked her way around the perimeter of a wedge of pizza—three big slices stuck together by the melted cheese. With a deft movement of the wrist, she lifted all three at once and dropped them down on two plates that she had arranged in front of her.

Jolly Trixie was just warming up. I could tell. She finished off the three pieces before I was halfway through my slice. I was just getting to the crust when she reached over and cut herself another wedge, finishing off the first pie. Within minutes, Pete arrived with the second pie. I went through the ritual of denuding two slices of pepperoni, gave one to Arnold and another to myself and watched as Jolly Trixie attacked the rest of the pie.

"Where did you go to school?" Arnold asked Trixie, curious about the rest of her life.

"Dropped out when I was 16," she said, "School bored me."

I didn't believe her. School probably was torture to her. Who could imagine teenagers tolerating a fat girl? She probably couldn't wait to reach the minimum age and quit.

"So, I went to work in Coney Island—washing dishes in a delicatessen. The pay wasn't good but the food was great—all the pastrami and French fries I could eat and all the sour pickles, too. I stayed there for five years, then moved to Atlantic City—where I worked in a pancake house, frying bacon for another four years. I moved into the rooming house on Beech Street about two months ago and here I am running my own business. How's that for a success story?"

Trixie was diving into the third pie now as I looked on in utter amazement. She offered us a couple of slices. I shook my head no. Arnold surprised me by taking one—holding out his hand as she forked one over. For a moment, he held on to her pinkie finger, gauging its girth.

They were staring at one another. His brown eyes meeting her blue eyes.

"I've got PLANS," Trixie said to Arnold. "I'm ambitious. I won't be here long if I can help it." She winked at Arnold as if to say, I can't tell you what I'm up to—but it's good.

Arnold winked back. "I thought I'd only be here a short while, too," he said. "But it didn't work out that way." He was biting into the slice, tomato sauce dripping from one corner of his mouth. "Beach towns have a way of holding on to you," he said.

I knew what he meant. There was something addictive about the sea air, the peeling paint, the splinters in your palm. Once you had drunk in the salt, it was hard to breathe anywhere else. Once you walked barefoot on the board-walk, it was hard to leave—even if you had to carry around a sharp tweezers for an emergency. I could get any splinter out, however small or deep. I kept a box full of tweezers in the cabinet, under my cash register, just in case.

"I can't imagine myself living far from the ocean," I said. Trixie and Arnold sat silent, almost in a trance. The pies were finished.

"Time for dessert," Trixie said, signaling for Pete. With her right hand, she made a circle in the air. Then, another.

"I just love his zeppoles," she said. The thought of a plate of hot dough, smothered with powered sugar, turned my stomach. But Arnold seemed into it.

"Haven't had a zeppole in years," Arnold said. I had never seen him eat one. He hated grease—or at least he always told me that he did.

The door to the pizza parlor opened and a gust of air swept through the room. You were used to this in a beach town where the sky blackened swiftly, and the surf got rough. Trixie became quiet, even reflective.

"All I have to do is keep eating," she said. "Keep myself from getting blue," she said.

"Everyone adored Jolly Trixie because she was FAT. She was FAMOUS." Trixie was guzzling her third Coke now, twirling the striped straw in her pudgy fingers.

"He just walked out," she said, not bothering to explain who he was. "I came home and he was gone. Toothbrush, shaving cream." For a moment, I thought she was going to cry.

"He loved my fat. The fatter, the better," he said. "But he left. No note. Nothing. Just walked out. Never heard from him again."

She lifted her straw out of the glass and tapped it on the table. She was working hard to change her mood. "You don't have to worry about me," Trixie said. "I've got BIG plans for my future. Big people have big plans!" She was back to her jolly self.

Pete arrived with a pyramid of zeppoles resting on a plate covered with wax paper. Trixie dove in first, polishing off two in seconds. Arnold followed her. He was smiling as he ate.

"Delicious," he said. "Just delicious."

Arnold had succumbed. He reached for a third zeppole before Trixie gulped down another two.

"Arnold," I said, "Aren't you pigging out?" He frowned at me, a harsh, mind-your-own business scowl.

"I know when I'm full," he said, talking to me but fixated on Trixie.

"Nine down and four to go," Trixie said, looking at Arnold. "It's your turn."

Arnold reached for two more zeppoles—pushing the remaining two in Trixie's direction.

"We did it," he said.

Trixie smiled her great big smile. Then, she laughed her great big laugh. Arnold laughed, too, a raucous laugh that I had never heard before, a deep-down-from-the-belly laugh that shocked me.

Trixie yawned and began to rub her eyes. She was full and sleepy.

"I'm exhausted," she said.

"Me, too," Arnold said. He stood up and brushed the crumbs off of his plaid shirt. "Never was a neat eater," he said.

"I'll walk you home," Arnold said, avoiding making eye contact with me.

Trixie struggled to get out of her chair, which had suddenly gotten too small for her.

"Thanks," she said. "I'd like that. I live in The Jefferson."

Arnold motioned for the check and he paid the bill. "It's on me, Trixie," he said, stopping her from handing him a few singles. "Welcome to the board-walk. Welcome to skeeball and Playworld. We're glad you're here."

Trixie blushed. I shivered.

The wind was blowing from the ocean as we walked toward The Jefferson.

"They're predicting a storm tomorrow," Arnold said. "There won't be many bathers. I used to think that I would get more business at Playworld when the water was rough—but I know better now. They just stay home."

We were standing in the lobby of The Jefferson. I hadn't been inside since my friend Margie moved out—about two years ago. The place looked even seedier than I remembered it. The green flowered wallpaper was peeling from the walls and the flowered carpet was frayed and dirty. There was a large plastic potted palm, tilted at an odd angle, stuck in a pink plastic pot. The place smelled of cigarette smoke. An old man sat rocking in a chair, wheezing as he slept.

"The rent's cheap and it's quiet," Trixie said, reading my mind. "It's hard to get better near the Boardwalk. Not much of a kitchen. Just a hot plate and a tiny fridge."

"Perfect for eating out," Arnold said.

"Perfect."

He reached for Trixie's hand and kissed it.

Trixie waddled up the stairs to her room, stopping on the fourth step to wave to Arnold and blow him a kiss. It flew through the air landing on his waiting lips.

Orphans' Day

August 1960

I HAD MY INSTRUCTIONS, straight from Mrs. Hutchinson. The boys, all 12 of them, were to be lined up by 7 AM, dressed in new white T-shirts with Mercy Orphanage printed in bold yellow letters and blue shorts. I was to see to it that their teeth were brushed and their hair combed. Mrs. Hutchinson did not want to be embarrassed.

I was to place a red lariat with a blue ID tag around each neck—to make sure that they did not get lost. The ID tag was also their free one-day pass to the beach and the boardwalk.

Everyone in town took pity on the orphans. They descended on the beach each August, their thin white bodies in need of sun and surf. The women lined up to be "mothers for a day" and the local teens helped out at the concessions and the rides. Each kid got a beach locker, a towel, and a donated bathing suit. There was free food—all you-could-eat—from a perfect menu of hot dogs, French fries, soda pop, ice cream, and candy. There were free games and free rides. You could spend the entire afternoon in the penny arcade seeking your fortune from The Answer Girl or getting dizzy on the whip in Playworld.

Most were city kids who did not understand the undertow of the ocean. To save them from drowning, the town fathers roped off a swimming area and hired extra lifeguards for the day.

We were to walk over to Playworld at noon where we would meet the thousands of other orphans, arriving in caravans of buses from 60 city orphanages. I was fourteen—the oldest boy at Mercy, having survived seven Orphans' Days. I knew the drill.

There was something terribly sad about Orphans' Day. At least I always felt that way. Oh, everyone was nice to you, too nice. Poor kid, their eyes said, no mother, no father, no home. Everywhere you went, those were the unspoken words. On the face of Jolly Trixie, selling hot dogs. In the eyes of Hymie at the greyhound arcade.

"Pick a prize from the top shelf," he would say, even when the kids were short 100 points.

I took home a leopard once that Mrs. Hutchinson rejected. "Too big," she said, waving her hand and pointing her finger to the stairway that led to the basement playroom. All donations went down there. Three-wheeled bicycles. Rusted tow trucks, missing their hitches. Dolls with no eyes. Two weeks before Christmas, the shopping bags would start arriving, left on our doorsteps like discarded newborns. Mothers were cleaning out their closets. Old junk had to make way for Santa's gifts. Mrs. Hutchinson wrote a thank-you note to each donor on pink stationery that smelled of honeysuckle.

I hated the thought of relegating the leopard to the basement. But down he went, next to a stuffed giraffe that Peter had won at skeeball last year.

By the time we marched over to Playworld, there were ten yellow buses in the parking lot and nearly 500 kids out on the street, making a racket. Arnold was standing by the entrance to Playworld, waving at me as I walked towards him.

"Biggest turnout ever," Arnold said, eyeing the crowd which continued to swell.

I wanted to cry but I didn't. This was supposed to be a happy day. But looking at the thousands of orphans made me sad. I was probably luckier than most of them. Arnold loved me—I was sure of that.

Arnold put his hand around my shoulder, patting me twice, as if to say, take it easy. I leaned backwards, resting my head for one moment on his strong chest. I could count on Arnold. He would never let me down, never.

I heard someone calling my name. Across the street stood Mrs. Hutchinson, dressed in white, a straw hat with a wide brim perched on top of her head. She was carrying a clipboard.

She gestured with her hand, a sure sign that I better hurry over or else. There was no fooling around with Mrs. H. You either did what she told you to do or you spent the rest of the day being punished. She could assign you cleaning the toilets or peeling potatoes. She could stand you in front of the old wooden ironing board with the torn and burnt cover and force you to iron the white shirts that we wore to church on Sunday morning.

I raced across the street, only to be handed the bathing suit list. Just the week before, we lined the boys up and measured their waists. Mrs. Hutchinson did not want one of her boys to lose his trunks in the ocean. Last year, a kid from the Bronx dove into a wave and emerged nude, his bathing suit sucked out with the undertow. There were whistles and loud applause as he ran for a towel, his penis hanging between his skinny white legs.

"Make sure that the suits fit," she said to me. "If you can fit your five fingers into the waist, it's too loose."

Once everyone had a suit, we changed in the locker rooms. Then, with striped towel in hand, we headed to the beach for a swim. There were six extra lifeguards on duty, one every fifteen feet of beach. Behind them, on the sand, were yellow life rafts and life preservers. I knew what it was like to be gasping for breath, desperate to come up for air. Arnold told me that it was worse if you tried to fight the ocean. The idea was to let it take you and release you. Fighting the undertow was a fatal mistake.

We Mercy kids were at an advantage. We lived by the ocean and understood its dangers. Most of us had scars from hitting the boulders on the jetties that were built to break the current and prevent erosion. It was best to swim far from the rocks, which were covered with slippery seaweed and which teemed with sea life. It was almost as dangerous to walk out on them. Mrs. Hutchinson forbade us from climbing them, although we had all broken her rules. Once, holding Arnold's hand, I walked to the end of the jetty on the beach by Playworld. The last few rocks were completely green and the waves hit them hard, sending up a plume of spray. Arnold was not afraid but I was, digging my nails into the underside of his palm. I almost slipped twice but Arnold, with his strong, muscular arms, held on to me.

The other kids lived in brick apartment buildings and played in tar-paved yards. The only water they knew came from fire hydrants. Their enemy was cars, which could hit them when they played stickball, racing in and out of parked cars on the city streets. Slippery rocks meant nothing to them. They had learned to swim in pools, where you could drown but where there were no currents, no waves, and no undertow. They thought that they were good swimmers. We knew better.

I was to be an extra pair of eyes, glued to the boys. Sure, there were lifeguards but they had hundreds of kids to watch, an impossible task. My job was to keep the Mercy boys in my sight at all times and to scream at any wise guy who drifted off from the group. Mrs. Hutchinson had drilled them all week at breakfast. Any boy who wandered away would be assigned to bathroom duty for a month. If you had to be rescued, you could be grounded for a year. Mrs. H sure knew how to instill fear. I was afraid of her eyes. When she stared at you, she looked like a volcano about to erupt. There was a hissing sound, like steam, exploding into the air. Then her words poured out, like hot lava searing your skin.

I blew my whistle, bought for me by Mrs. H because it sounded like a whippoorwill. The boys knew that sound. Mrs. H had a phonograph recording of the bird singing and she played it in the lunchroom. When you heard the whirring chirp, you were to freeze up and listen and wait.

"Waist deep and no deeper," I called out, "and stay in the roped off area. Keep away from the rocks and no diving down and holding your breath for as long as you can."

Peter, who was the ringleader of mischief, wasn't paying attention. I could see that his eyes were fogged over. He was kicking the sand with his foot, as if to say, Oh yeah. That's what you think. I don't have to listen to you. Peter spent hours in detention writing, "I promise never to steal pretzels from the candy store. I promise never to smoke a cigarette under the boardwalk." His promises were worth as much as the wooden nickels that Beverly gave out in skeeball. Larger than a real nickel, on one side they had an outline of a buffalo that looked more like a horse. Printed on the other side, in block letters were the words: FUN IN THE SUN—THE BOARDWALK. The Mercy kids collected them, washed up on the beach, discarded on benches. I don't know why. You couldn't cash them in for anything, although Peter said they were perfect for poker chips.

Where and when Peter played poker was a mystery to me. He had his secrets. I watched him wriggling in place. I was rooting for him, hoping that he would beat Mrs. H at her own game. I was too timid to act out. The thought of losing my visiting privileges with Arnold was more than I could bear.

I read out the instructions that Mrs. H had written in black ink, her large bold letters bouncing from the page. Everyone was to follow the same schedule. After the ocean swim, we were to meet for lunch on the boardwalk, right in front of Jolly Trixie's hot dog stand, which stood to the left of the entrance to the skeeball arcade. Lunch was two hot dogs, washed down with soda pop. Trixie was Beverly's friend, which meant that she would give us three hot dogs, if we could actually eat that many. I couldn't. Not if I wanted to leave room for ice cream and cotton candy, which I did. After lunch, there was a ceremony with a speech by the mayor and welcoming words from Mrs. H who was the chairman of the Orphans' Homes Regional Association. What a marvelous day it was, she told the crowd. How fortunate you orphans are to benefit from the generosity of the boardwalk. Then, she lowered her head and asked everyone to thank God. I heard Peter say, "For what," and watched him spit on the boardwalk. The other boys put their hands together and stared at the ground. Huddled together, we looked like penguins about to make our annual march to the sea.

Thankfully, the speeches were short and we headed over to the penny arcade and Playworld, where Arnold was determined to give us so many rides that we would leave dizzy, weaving our way back to the beach for an afternoon dip in the ocean. I loved the Answer Girl in the arcade. Her eyes were bright blue and her lashes black and long. A paisley scarf was draped around her head and shoulders and long gold earrings swung from her ears. Insert a penny in the slot and out came your yellow, orange or pink fortune card, your destiny. I had read about the Romany Gypsies who wandered from country to country, stealing your money. They were tricksters and thieves, who carried long daggers. Their women wore full red and yellow skirts. They flirted with the men. The children picked your pockets.

The Answer Girl on the boardwalk was safe. Made of wax and locked in a glass cage, she could not steal your money. We plied her with pennies. Where would we go after Mercy? No one had adopted us. You will lead a long and fulfilling life, my orange card with the picture of the gypsy on it, told me. You will be rich. You will have a big family. You will travel round the globe. She rarely handed out bad news. Once, Jimmy cried the whole day after he read his fortune: You will have bad luck for the next month, the card said. Jimmy locked himself in his room. Only Mrs. Hutchinson could convince him to come out.

Arnold was flooded with kids at Playworld. There were long lines for the bumper cars. You had to be 36 inches tall to ride and the kids whose heads did not reach the blue line were inconsolable when they were denied entry. Arnold tried to comfort them by placing them in the jeweled saddles of the white horses that led the parade on the carousel. Only the youngest kids stopped crying. The bigger boys got back on line, this time wearing three caps to make themselves taller.

The skeeball arcade was jammed, too, and Beverly had acquired two teenage girl helpers, volunteers from the local high school. They stood behind the prize cases, barely controlling the kids who were clamoring for their rewards. Most popular were the made-in-Japan plaster kewpie dolls, dressed in brocade kimonos with contrasting red and blue obis, their slanting eyes edged in black ink. The girls traded them. For one coupon, you could get a folding fan, made of tissue paper that was covered with dragons. The boys loved the shiny shooter marbles and the cap guns, which we were not allowed to bring back into the orphanage. We hid them in secret places, retrieving them for shootouts.

Beverly had closed down her cash register for the day so that she was free to move from lane to lane giving professional advice. Twist your wrist, she told a boy, whose ball kept falling short, landing in the 10-point circle. Aim high, above the 50-point circle, and the ball will curve down into it, she told another kid who kept hitting the 30-points ring. When they finally hit the 50-point circle, Beverly made sure to give out double tickets. After all, for most of the kids, this was their only beach day and it wasn't easy to rack up the 30 coupons you needed to claim one of the prizes on the top shelf. Beverly told me that she had ordered a double shipment of prizes for Orphans' Day. Last year, the most popular prize was a tiny radio, the size of a postcard, in green or red bakelite, which cost 100 coupons. She'd had 10 on hand and she'd wished that she had more. This year, she had ordered 50.

By late afternoon, the kids were reassembled on the beach, their arcade treasures stored on the yellow buses. They were waiting for me to blow my bird whistle for that penultimate swim of the day. The tide was pulling out and a scalloped line of shells and seaweed already could be seen dotting the sand. The surf was rough and a succession of waves crashed against the jetty.

"No one is to walk on the rocks," I called out to my boys. "They're much too slippery." I was probably asking for trouble. When Mrs. H said that something was forbidden, our first response was to defy her. Not that we often did. But down deep there was the impulse to break loose. We were sick of rules. We made our beds hospital-style, with the sheets folded crisply at the corners. We all sported the same haircut. We all wore the same white socks, a gift from Sol, the sock manufacturer who gave us $200 worth of socks every year and took a tax deduction for $1,000. The socks slipped down, bunching up in our shoes. We hated them. But Mrs. H said, "Don't look a gift horse in the mouth." These socks, she insisted, were good enough for orphans. In fact, Mrs. H was sure that just about anything was good enough for us—shoes that pinched and shirts that gave us hives. An orphan, she told us, should always be grateful.

That was pretty hard to swallow. I wasn't grateful for the lumpy mattress that I slept on. All night long, I shifted from lump to lump, trying to make myself comfortable. What a joke! Here I was giving orders to the boys when I wanted to rebel myself.

The boys dropped their towels in the sand and made a mad dash for the water. There were several hundred kids in the ocean now, tossing striped beach balls back and forth and diving under the surf, only to resurface, their mouths open, gasping for air. The chief lifeguard blew his whistle, motioning for the kids to come closer to shore.

"No beach balls," he screamed, through his megaphone. Within seconds, the balls lay on the dunes, and the boys were back in the ocean.

I scanned the horizon—watching for a big wave that signaled trouble. The outgoing tide and the strong southwesterly wind made the sea especially rough. The effects of Tropical Storm Irene could still be felt, although the storm was already several hundred miles north up the coast. The beach had been closed for three days when the storm passed through.

Peter was the furthest out. A strong swimmer, he dove through the highest waves effortlessly. The other boys hung back, frightened by the pull of the current.

"Scaredy Cat!" Peter cried, taunting Charles, who stood in waist deep water. When Charles was little, he was even afraid of the bathtub. He'd cry when the water rose above his belly button.

"I'm not moving," Charles screamed back at Peter.

Peter responded by diving under a huge wave which rolled toward the shore menacingly. The other boys ran from it, heading toward the shallow water for safety. Charles reached me first, panting from the run.

"Killer wave," he said. "I thought I was gonna die."

I patted Charles on the shoulder and looked out on the horizon. There was no sign of Peter—not directly in front of me and not on the jetties to my left.

"Peter," I screamed. "Has anyone seen Peter?" No one answered.

The monster wave had crashed on the beach, leaving a momentary calm on the ocean surface. Far out on the horizon, another wave was forming.

"Help, help," I screamed, gesturing with my hand to the chief lifeguard.

"Peter, Peter," I kept screaming but there was neither a splash nor a sound.

Within seconds, the beach was closed down and the lifeguards sprang into action, two each in an inflatable raft, paddling out to sea.

"He was there," I kept screaming, pointing to the spot in the ocean where I had last seen Peter take his dive.

They paddled back and forth over the area, frequently diving down to look for him. Five minutes. Ten minutes. Fifteen minutes.

One of the lifeguards on the beach picked up the megaphone and told all of the kids to go back to the locker room, change, and board their buses. Orphans' Day at the beach is officially over, he said.

The Mercy boys did not want to leave. They were clustered around me, their thin bodies shivering in the late afternoon breeze.

"Mrs. H is sure going to be angry at Peter," Charles said.

"How can she be angry at him," Robert answered, "if he's drowned?"

We sat in a circle on the beach, staring at the lifeguards who were rowing back and forth. The ocean was getting rougher and the current stronger. A Coast Guard motorboat with radar arrived to help with the search.

"We probably won't find the body till tomorrow," I heard one of them call to the other. "The kid will wash in with the tide."

The thought of Peter washing in with the driftwood and the clamshells made me cry. Within seconds, the other boys were crying, too. Peter was our tough guy, the kid who was going to make it outside. We were all counting on him.

Mrs. H would blame me. I was sure of that. "Why weren't you watching him?" she would ask me. "I should have known better than to trust the boys to you," she would say.

I kept thinking about what I would tell her. But no matter what I would say, it would not help.

Mrs. H came running toward us, her shoes in hand.

"That Peter," she said. "Always causing trouble. Leave it to him to drown!"

She came over to me and, without saying a word, removed the bird whistle from around my neck. Then she blew it loudly. "Time to go home," she said.

The Answer Girl

Summer 1961

BENNY SAT ON A PILLOW, facing a mound of pennies that were piled high on several sheets of newspaper. Earlier that morning, he had dumped several thousand on yesterday's paper. He was determined to count every one, filling the red paper 50-cent sleeves that he had gotten from the bank by the railroad station. It was a two-week project. Maybe longer.

This was the summer of the big announcement: the arrival of the nickel arcade. The story had already appeared in the boardwalk newsletter: "Penny Arcade Is Up to a Five and Dime," the headline read. "I never thought I would live to see this day," a 60-year-old homemaker lamented, adding that her entire childhood was shaped by the mayonnaise jar full of pennies that she saved to use in the arcade.

Although the sign out front still screamed Penny Arcade in bright blue letters one foot high, balls of red light flickering on the blue, there was only one machine left that actually still took pennies. Benny had converted them all over the winter, changing the coin slots to fit nickels and dimes. Only The Answer Girl resisted; its mechanism unyielding to inflation. He had removed the tiny screws on the coin box but had been unable to make the conversion. After several frustrating hours, he decided that it would remain unaltered, a relic of the arcade's history. There she stood, a proud woman who knew all the answers.

Benny played The Answer Girl all the time. You never could get enough answers. He had his questions: Would he drown in the ocean? Would someone drop a lighted cigarette and burn down his arcade? Would Marilyn leave him for Jack, who smoked big cigars and wore flowered ties? Jack worked at the poker arcade and he was always winking at her. The Answer Girl had her questions and her answers. It didn't matter that hers were different. There was always a way to interpret the words, to apply them to his life.

When he turned the knob to select the question, "Will I Find True Hap-

131

piness in Life?" the Answer Girl nodded her wax head and a yellowed card popped out from the answer box: "You Have Found True Happiness Already," it said. He had just had a big fight with Marilyn. The Answer Girl told him that he had better make up with her fast.

When he selected the question, "Will My Business Prosper?" another card appeared: "Decisive Action Is Called For. Be Bold." Benny understood the meaning immediately. It was time to raise his prices, abandoning pennies for nickels and dimes. So, he gave The Answer Girl a place of honor, standing her just to the right of the old cash register, which was plastered with lucky one dollar bills. In a jam, he could reach over and stroke the glass case. In a pinch, he could lean over and ask a question.

The kids weren't much interested in her answers. They gathered around the machine that shot bullets at wild bears. If you were deft, you could kill a dozen bears in a few seconds. It was a macho competition with the bigger boys outshooting the little ones. When you hit a bear, there was the loud BOOM of a gunshot as the bear exploded and vanished. Lights flashed too, celebrating the kill. There was something primal about the game–a modern version of the cave man on a hunt. The boys screamed. They jumped up and down. The wooden floor in the arcade shook.

Shooting balls into targets was almost as popular as killing the bears. It was a game of skill. If you were clumsy, it was best to wrap yourself in a fluffy towel and sunbathe on the beach. The arcade was for athletes, real boys who could flex their biceps and wink at the girls.

Benny dusted the glass case of The Answer Girl every morning. He wanted to cheer her up. Her brown eyes had lost their luster and her pink lipstick had faded. One pearl earring hung lopsided on her left lobe. Locked in a glass cage, how happy could she be? Her yellow light rarely went on and she could hear the sounds of the boys whooping out loud as they took aim. Those kids had all the answers.

Only the old timers came by for her advice. Beverly was a regular—stopping by on her lunch break from the skeeball arcade to feed pennies into the slot. She had her favorites. "Does He Really Love Me?" That was the BIG one. She'd turn that knob at least once a week, glancing from side to side so that no one could see her reading the slightly wrinkled card: "More Than You Think He Does!" The Answer Girl never frowned. She never grimaced. All she did was smile—no matter what answer she gave.

Arnold was a regular, too, stopping by on Friday afternoons to schmooze about business on the boardwalk.

"Too many rainy days," Arnold complained, reaching into his pocket and fishing out a handful of pennies. "Business has been terrible."

"Yep," Benny said, scanning his nearly empty penny arcade. When it rained the boys were grounded. "Last Tuesday was a bomb. I was the only one in the arcade."

Arnold dropped a penny into the slot and turned the knob to his favorite question # 3: "Will I Make Money This Year?" He had been surviving by withdrawing money from the bank every week but his account was getting low. The rate he was going, he would have nothing left by early spring. What would he do then? Playworld could be boarded up for the winter and he could hibernate for a few months but reopening the amusement park meant an infusion of new funds for paint and lumber. Winters by the ocean were hard. The wind whipped across the park, tearing the canvas covers. The rain and snow rotted the wood and peeled last year's paint. His line of credit at the hardware store was already at its limit.

Last week, The Answer Girl told him that there were BIG hurdles before him; the week before that she warned him to be cautious. "Don't Listen To Strangers," she said.

Today, her words were ominous: "You Face Two Paths. One Will Lead to Success. The Other to Failure. Make the Right Choice!" Arnold squinted at the words and shivered. The least she could have done was to tell him which way to turn.

"Nothing good here," he said to Benny.

"She hasn't been very helpful to me either," Benny said, "She owes me one. I could have thrown her out." He laughed, a big heavy laugh, quickly followed by a sigh. "Who but a fool would have kept her?"

"We're both fools," Arnold said. "Only fools would be trying to make a living on the boardwalk. What's the use of hanging on by a thread? Don't you ever think of boarding your place up for good? All you'd have to do is wake up one morning, padlock the metal gates, roll up the awning, and take down the sign. There has to be another life for us out there."

Benny grimaced. He had been thinking those very thoughts for years without coming up with the right answer—if there was one. He was a good carpenter but he didn't know if he wanted to work that hard. He had gotten used to the rhythm of the arcade business—a three-week spruce-up in the late spring, followed by a busy summer, leaving him a quiet fall and an even quieter winter. Carpenters built houses in the snow. He had seen them nailing up sheathing, fighting off the south wind from the ocean which threatened to blow them from their ladders. They'd meet at the coffee shop. Carl was 23 years old but he was always talking about how sore his right arm was from hammering. Bill was 30 but he complained about his lower back. It was shot, he said, from lifting five-gallon cans of roofing tar. "Those babies weigh fifty pounds. More than both of my kids," he'd always tell him.

Arnold understood. Work had a different definition on the boardwalk. He painted yellow daisies on choo-choo trains and white clouds floating in a blue sky. He tied new silver fringe on the lead horse of the carousel, braiding the ends artistically. He patched the holes in the tank that held the boats, caulking the seams and painting the bottom a deep green-blue like the ocean. On the stairs up to the ride, he drew crabs crawling their way to the top. The kids counted them as they mounted.

It was work and it wasn't. He was getting tired of eating peanut butter and jelly sandwiches for lunch and of counting and rolling pennies when he came to the end of the month and was short a few dollars. But Arnold wasn't eager to try life outside.

Benny reached over for the worn deck of cards that sat on the shelf above the cash register. Whenever Arnold visited, they always played gin rummy. Until recently, they had been running even. Lately, however, Benny was on a roll.

"My luck's changing," Arnold said as he shuffled the deck. "I can't be a loser all my life." He dealt out the cards, looked down at his hand and saw that he had nothing.

"Not bad," Benny said, discarding a three of clubs.

Arnold knew that Benny's not bad meant just the opposite. He had a good, maybe a great hand. When Benny said that something was passable, you'd better watch out.

Arnold picked a four of hearts and discarded it, only to have Benny scoop it up.

"Thanks," he said, running his fingers along the edges of his cards. It was almost a caress.

Ten minutes later, Benny said gin and the game was over. He took down the yellow legal pad and added his victory to their scorecard.

"You're down by four," he said. Benny slapped Arnold on the back. It was a friendly blow. "Cheer up," it said.

After Arnold left to return to Playworld, Benny walked back to the washroom, filled a pail with water and a splash of Spic and Span, and grabbed a mop. Every Friday afternoon, like the Jews scouring their houses before the Sabbath, he mopped the arcade floor.

He dunked the mop in the pail, twisted the strands with his hands to ring out the water, and began to wash the linoleum, its tic-tac-toe pattern faded but still visible. There was a slight dimple in the center of each of the red o's, leaving a puddle of water on every circle. Chunks of yellow were missing from some of the x's. As a result, some x's had become v's, other's y's. Bobby had written his name with a permanent black marker on one square. Another was inscribed with a heart bearing the words *Johnny Loves Maria, Summer 1955.*

Benny remembered them. They were always making out behind the machine where you could shoot rifle bullets at the Indians. Maria, with curly black hair and an Italian last name and Johnny, blue-eyed and blonde, an Irish kid from the West End. She wore his high school ring around her neck. Maria was now a waitress in the pizza parlor in town. He had seen her there a month ago. Her hair was streaked with red and her full lips were painted red. There was no wedding band. He wanted to ask her about Johnny but didn't.

"How's the arcade?" she asked him. "Still alive?"

"Just about," Benny answered. It was a tough question—one Benny asked himself and The Answer Girl almost every day. Marilyn was ready to pack up and leave. Boardwalk life bored her.

"Gimme five good reasons why we should stay?" she kept asking him. Benny could only come up with two. "It's the only world I know," he told her. "And, I don't think I could breathe without the salt air."

"You can learn to breathe anywhere," Marilyn said, "even in a coal mine. I'm telling you, Benny, this can't go on. One of these days, I'm out of here."

She threatened but Benny didn't take her seriously. Marilyn had no prospects, at least none that Benny knew of. She worked at the telephone company, on one of those big switchboards with 12 incoming trunk lines and 75 extensions. At the end of her junior year in high school, she had dropped out, bored with her courses. She and her boyfriend at the time, a 21-year-old guy who worked as a mechanic's helper at the garage in town, headed out west. She told everybody that they would never see her again.

One year later, Marilyn returned. Rumors spread that she had had an abortion and that the guy was nowhere to be found. Marilyn got the phone company job and moved into her parents' apartment on the boardwalk. When her father retired and her parents fled to Florida, she inherited it with its flowered linoleum and yellow and black tile bathroom. That's where she lived ever since.

Lately, however, Marilyn had been going into the city on her day off. She said that she was going shopping but she rarely came home with purchases. Benny was worried that there was another guy. The Answer Girl said no but Benny wasn't sure. Arnold told him that he thought he saw her one day walking on the beach with a man he did not recognize. When asked to describe him, all Arnold said was that he was tall and thin.

Benny looked at his paunch and reflected on how often Marilyn would punch him in the gut. "Look at that flab," she would say. It was a light jab but she did it often enough to worry him.

Always, it was the same old question: Was there life after the boardwalk? Everything seemed dull in comparison. Paved. Predictable. Paltry. That was the real reason he had never left. If you were lucky, you won a prize. It did not matter how cheap it was. It did not matter if it fell apart the next day.

The kids were clustered around the bear game, fighting for turns. Jimmy was the biggest and he was always first. No one disputed that. If you did, you could end up with a black eye. Tommy, his henchman, was second. Scrappy and mean, Tommy was only too willing to kick you in the shins if you got in his way. Pete was third. He removed a wad of pink bubble gum from his mouth and stuck it on the glass case of The Answer Girl when it was his turn to shoot.

"Don't do that," Benny yelled at him, rushing over to remove the gum.

"Piece of junk," Pete said. "It just takes up room."

Benny knew better than to pick a big fight. He needed their business. So, he went back to his desk. He could hear them snickering. They played for about an hour and left together. Pete punched The Answer Girl as he walked out.

It was already six in the evening and Benny was late for a date with Marilyn. He shut down the lights of the arcade, locked the front door and set the alarm. Then, he headed down the ramp of the boardwalk on his way to Marilyn's apartment. After pasta at the restaurant, they were going bowling. Benny's lower back had been killing him lately and his right thumb ached too. But Marilyn liked to bowl so he had not said a word.

Marilyn served them from the kitchen, lasagna with a side order of meatballs and spaghetti. Mario, the owner, stopped by to talk.

Same old question. How's business?

Same old answer. So-so. Holding on.

Mario waved No when Benny tried to pay for dinner.

"Just tip the waitress!" he said, laughing.

By the time they reached Bowl-Right, their lane was ready. Lucky Nine. They always played that lane. Marilyn had her own ball and her own shoes. Her first ball was a strike.

"Gonna break 200 tonight," Marilyn said.

They played three games. Benny kept rolling the ball into the gutter. Marilyn kept getting strikes. When they paused for a beer, Benny could hear sirens outside. The police station was around the corner. Two cars, sirens blasting, took off for somewhere.

"What's up?" Benny asked Jim, the bartender.

"Nothing much," he answered. Jim was a member of the police auxiliary. If something big had happened, say a murder, the sergeant would page him.

They played one more game and headed back to Benny's apartment, around the corner from the arcade. As they walked up the block, Benny could see flashing red lights from a police car, parked by the boardwalk.

He ran toward the police car.

"Just the guy we were waiting for," Sergeant Riley said.

"Someone broke into your arcade. Cash register drawer is empty. So is the prize case. But everything else looks OK."

The lock on the front door was smashed. Benny flipped the light switch and turned on the arcade lights. Two hundred dollars was missing from the cash register although the thief had left the change. The stuffed animals were gone from the top shelf of the prize case.

"By the time we got here," Riley said, "the place was empty."

"Probably escaped on the beach," Benny said, looking across the boardwalk, to the ocean beyond.

Suddenly, Benny shivered. Something wasn't right. He turned once again to survey the arcade. The Answer Girl was gone; only the stand and the glass case remained. He ran down the steps to the beach, flashlight in hand.

The tide was starting to come in and the surf was rough. Marilyn followed as did Sergeant Riley.

Within minutes, Benny saw her lying in the sand. Her lovely head was decapitated from her shoulders and one eye was stabbed clear through with a stick. He stared at her. She stared back with her remaining eye. Who had done this to her and why so brutal? Decapitation. Mutilation. Who would tell him what to do? Who would answer his questions?

There would be no more flashing lights. No more blinking of her eyes. Only the rat-tat-tat of guns shooting in the arcade.

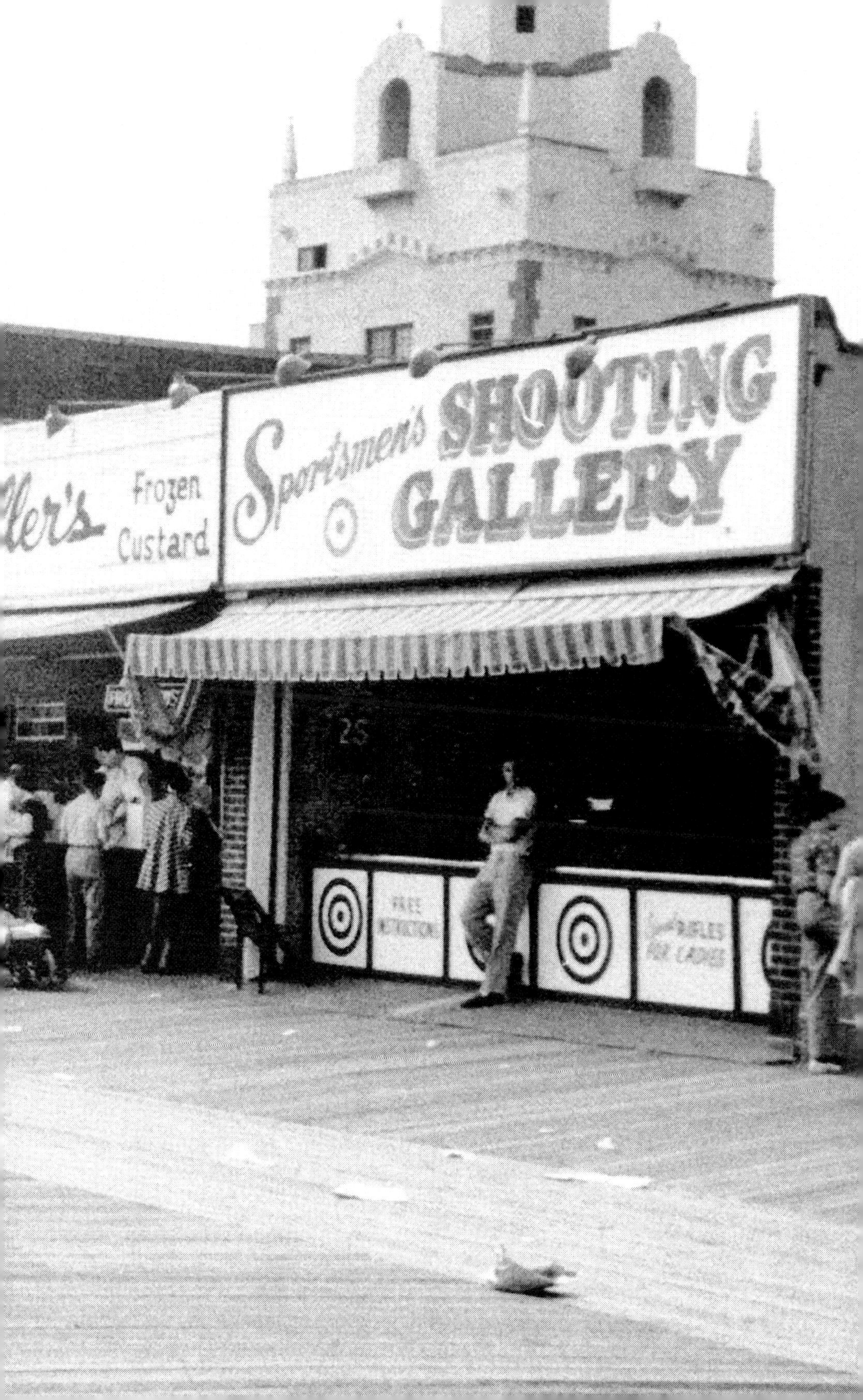
ller's
Frozen Custard
Sportsmen's SHOOTING GALLERY
25

Working the Switchboard

ONE WRONG MOVE AND YOU COULD DISCONNECT THEM. That's what George Fowler told me on my first day of work. All you had to do was pull out the black trunk lines before you thought about it and it was all over. Harry Berman would be disconnected from Charles, his stockbroker and all hell would break loose. Berman would run down the hotel stairs and call for me at the front desk.

"What happened, Susan?" he'd scream. "I was in the middle of a deal. Get Charles back on the line."

I'd mumble something about an accident and redial Charles or Charlie Boy, as Berman liked to call him. Berman would race back up to his second floor, ocean-front suite to catch the call on the first ring. But he wouldn't let me forget about it.

"Watch what you're doing or no tip," he'd say the next day, on his way to the dining room for breakfast.

"Yesterday was a $5,000 day. I was a big-time winner."

This was my third summer working at The Franklin, a three-story yellow brick building on Beech Street. All of the best rooms had views of the Atlantic and of the boardwalk. The guests were first-in-the-family-to-make-it-big businessmen with their wives and kids who were out at the beach for the summer. They had abandoned their homes in Brooklyn, Queens, and the Bronx for the sea air.

The wives played canasta under an umbrella on the beach while the kids dug sand castles. The men played gin rummy in the card room and swam twice a day, their skinny white legs a sure give-away that they were not locals. They'd speak to their brokers all day long, depending on me to hook them up.

I knew the names of their girlfriends too. Sally and Barbara and Roberta and Doris, who doubled as a secretary. All they had to say was "Call Sally" and

I would dial the number. I had them memorized.

My friend Beverly had gotten me the job. She knew George Fowler who owned The Franklin with his brother Sam. Beverly told George that I was her best friend, which wasn't exactly true. She said that I was very reliable and that I knew how to keep my mouth shut–another big lie.

I told Beverly everything. How Harry had a three-year affair going on with Roberta who ran the newsstand concession in Harry's office building. Roberta met him at The Parker Hotel every Wednesday at 1 PM. I knew the room number: 17. Harry bought Roberta a diamond ring from his friend Nathan who had a booth in the 47th Street Diamond Arcade. I had never seen the ring but I knew how much it cost. Two thousand dollars.

Beverly loved the gossip. All I had to do, I explained to her, was to leave the switch open and I could eavesdrop on the conversation. I had to be quiet, though; a sneeze could give me away. Once I did cough, only to cover the accident by interrupting the conversation to say, "Oops, sorry, I must have clicked on to the wrong line." That was an excuse that you could not use too often.

The wives had their fun too. Harry's wife Carole had bleached blonde hair and long red nails. Their daughter Flora went to day camp at Sand and Surf, three blocks away. The camp bus picked her up every morning at 8:00, just as I was arriving. Flora always waved to me. She wanted me to teach her to work the switchboard.

Harry took the 8:28 train to the City every day except Friday. He'd wait with Flora, then head off in the hotel van to catch his train. Carole leaned out her bedroom window, watching. Five minutes after they both were gone, she'd ring me.

"Get me Sid," she said. Sid was the maitre d' who controlled seating in the dining room. If you weren't nice to him, you ended up next to the swinging doors that led to the kitchen. Or worse, right across from the entrance to the men's and women's bathrooms.

Sid told me to put Carole through, no matter how busy he was and what meal was being served. Eight-thirty was a quiet time. Breakfast was winding down and prep for lunch not quite starting up. I knew that Carole was giving Sid the all-clear sign.

I was the only one who knew about their affair, besides Beverly who thought that Sid was a fool.

"If I ever caught Arnold cheating on me, I'd wring his neck," Beverly told me one evening as we wound down over a beer at McCabe's, a neighborhood hangout in the West End. McCabe's drew regulars who hit the bar in between work and home. By the time they left, they'd squandered a day's paycheck on cheap beer.

Beverly and I met there every Thursday night. It was our girls' night out ritual, a chance for her to catch up on the intrigues at The Franklin and for me to listen in on the ups and downs of life with Arnold. They got along, most of the time, Beverly assured me, except when Arnold pressured her to adopt Joey or when Arnold, frayed by a day at Playworld, dreamed of fleeing the board-walk. Then, life would explode like fireworks.

I was divorced for seven years, having dumped my first husband Saul when I understood that he would never stop drinking. It was a clean break, no kids and no money.

Beverly and I bonded immediately. I was a good listener, always up to hearing about the latest round at home. I knew the truth about men. They were babies. They needed to be pampered and they whined when they didn't get their way.

"Arnold's in a mood," Beverly said as she sipped her second beer. "It's Joey this and Joey that. 'Poor kid in the orphanage. We've got to rescue him.' It's driving me crazy." Beverly took a gulp and waited for me to respond.

"Children are a BIG responsibility," I said. "Best thing in the world that ever happened to me was that Saul and I never had kids. We were much too selfish to be good parents. You and Arnold seem different, though."

Beverly shook her head. "Might be right for Arnold but not for me," she said. "Kids are great at the arcade but not in my home."

All hell had broken loose at The Franklin. Harry had left for work and realized he had forgotten his office keys. He returned to the hotel to get them and let himself into his room only to find Carole and Sid nude in bed. The screaming could be heard in the card room, which was located in the east build-ing.

"Get the hell out of here," Harry screamed at Sid. "I'm gonna have you fired." After a minute or so, the time it took to pull on his pants, the door slammed. No one saw Sid for the rest of the day.

"What happened to Carole?" Beverly asked. "Didn't Harry explode at her?

"She came to dinner as usual, dressed in an orange polka-dot outfit. Harry led her in like a clipped poodle on a leash. Flora walked beside them, dressed in hot pink.

* * * * * * * * *

My fingers ached from a week's worth of pushing and pulling the trunk lines and from scribbling phone messages on pink slips. Edna would be late for her mah jong date with Clara. Bernice saw a fabulous tweed suit in Ohrbach's, perfect for Paula.

Celeste's son was turning seven. She asked me to dial Playworld. "I'm thinking of having a birthday party at Playworld for David," she told me as I rang the number. Arnold picked up. I was about to flick the switch when I heard Celeste say, "George will be away on business this weekend and David's sleeping at his grandparents."

I could hear Arnold's breathing, heavy and rapid.

"Not a good idea," Arnold said finally, his voice wavering. "A beach town is a very small place. Keeping a secret here is like trying to hold sand in your fingers."

"Meet me on Saturday night, after you close up," she said. "Under the boardwalk at Lincoln Avenue. It's deserted."

Arnold did not answer and I understood why. He was thinking of Beverly who would throw him out if she caught him with another woman and of Joey who needed a home which Beverly could give him.

"Come'on," Celeste said. "You said that I'm beautiful. You told me that I remind you of Betty Grable."

Before Arnold could answer, George entered the office and I clicked the switch closed, fearful that he would speak to me. I was dying to hear Arnold's answer but I just couldn't take the chance.

I definitely wasn't going to tell Beverly about Celeste's call to Arnold. Some things are best left alone.

* * * * * * * * *

"What are you doing Saturday night?" Beverly asked me. Her question shook me up.

"Nothing," I said, waiting for her reply.

"Arnold's taking Joey out for dinner, just the two of them. It's a chance to find out what's really on the kid's mind. Some times Joey seems so sad. It can't be easy living at the orphanage."

I nodded sympathetically but all I could think about was Celeste. Was Arnold lying to Beverly? Had he set up an under-the-boardwalk rendezvous using Joey as the excuse?

Beverly and I decided to meet at Russo's at 8 PM. It was a neighborhood restaurant with vinyl booths, stained with the remnants of Frankie's red sauce. Frankie was the second generation in the family to run the place and he made sure that the five entrees on the menu stayed the same. Spaghetti. Linguini. Manicotti. Veal Parmigiana. Meat Balls. We would wash it down with Chianti, carrying the bottles home as souvenirs.

I spent the week waiting and worrying. Celeste did not call Arnold, at least not when I was on switchboard duty. I spent most of the week calling the guest list for Harry's mother's 90th birthday party. Carole buzzed me thirty times a day with new names. They had rented out the hotel ballroom for the celebration and Harry had given Carole the assignment—her penance, perhaps for getting caught with Sid.

"I'll give you a big tip when this is over," she said to me one morning, embarrassed that she was calling me again. She wanted my opinion on the flower arrangements, daisies dyed bright pink and orange in yellow baskets.

"Do you think they're too loud?" she asked me. I knew better than to tell her the truth.

"They're so cheerful," I said, "after all it is a 90th birthday." The menu was equally ridiculous: chopped liver on saltines, a salad of cubed red Jell-0 and iceberg lettuce, and chicken chow mein. There would be a champagne toast and strawberry shortcake.

Carole went back and forth about the chow mein, wavering between it and meat loaf with onion gravy.

"Everyone loves meat loaf," Carole said, "especially older women. It's easy to chew when you have false teeth."

"Chow mein's more exotic," I said. "Meat loaf is boring." Carole was a wreck. When she stopped by the front desk and asked for change, I noticed that two fingernails were bitten down to the quick. There were dark circles under her eyes and her blonde bouffant had fallen flat.

"Can't wait until this is over," she said. "Harry makes me give him a report every hour. He's driving me nuts!"

I gave Beverly a vivid account of the party planning on Saturday when we met at Russo's. Within seconds, the waiter took our order and we were drinking Chianti.

"They're on the main course right now," I said. "I can just see the sauce dripping down their chins."

Beverly laughed. "Have pity," she said. "It's not nice to make fun of old people."

Working the switchboard at the hotel had definitely affected me. For a kid who loved her maternal grandmother, I had become cynical about old folks. They asked me the same thing four times a day. They told the same stale jokes. They were bad tippers. They gave out smells—mouth odor, body odor. I could see the same thing happening to me and I didn't like it. Better to die in your sleep than to grow old and smell.

"Old or young, you're needy," Beverly said. By the look on her face, I could tell that she was thinking of Joey who, so she thought, was off having dinner with Arnold. Or were they?

"We're all needy," I said, trying to comfort her. "I need a new job. You need Arnold. Everyone at the hotel needs something, usually from me. I'm the one they call. I'm Queen of the Switchboard. The woman you call when you're needy. Me." My voice choked a bit as I spit out the last phrase. I was good at my job but I resented it too. I was supposed to a technician but I had become a lifeline.

"They'd be lost without me, really. Ten times a day. Twenty calls to a doctor. Advice on the side effects of a new prescription. How to handle a husband. Or a grown daughter who was rebelling late in life. Who to put in their wills?

Beverly laughed. "You love it, Susan. You're complaining but you love it. You're playing God! Think of the power you have over their lives! You can save them from themselves."

I was about to answer her — to tell her that nothing could save them from themselves, when the restaurant door opened. Arnold entered, his arm around Joey's shoulder. Joey was smiling. He saw us immediately and came over to the table.

"Imagine meeting you two ladies here," he said.

Beverly gave me a funny look and then a wink. "We've just finished our drinks," she said. "You can have our table."

Arnold smiled at Beverly. I could tell that he was grateful to her for leaving.

"What's new at the hotel?" he asked me, as we paid our check and began to go.

"Not much to report," I said. "Same old. Same old. Beverly will fill you in."

Beverly and I stood up to give Arnold and Joey our seats. Arnold kissed Beverly and Beverly kissed Joey. Within seconds, we were outside, the salty smell of the sea in our nostrils.

"How about pizza?" Beverly asked.

I nodded yes, as we walked together, arm in arm.

Miss Lydia's Dance Studio

1 9 6 9

IT WAS THREE STEPS BELOW GROUND–not really in the basement–according to Miss Lydia who always sported a smile that revealed her white teeth and whose bangs were cut in an arc across her broad forehead. Still, it was low enough to be endangered when the fall hurricanes swept across the island, wind whipping the surf, ocean and bay meeting in the middle of the narrow streets.

That was a time when the sound of sump pumps could be heard straining, and the black hoses lay curled on the sandy concrete, belching water. Three feet and more of murky water, black sludge that ruined books and photographs, and left clothing smelling forever of sea and mildew.

Miss Lydia was a firm believer in bleach. A cup of Clorox, diluted in a gallon of water, could work wonders, especially if the scrubbing was done by hand, with an old toothbrush. In her pink and grey bathroom, she kept a dozen or so well-worn toothbrushes in a plastic pail which sported a picture of a mouth with a full set of teeth through which she had drawn a large, black X.

Every time I saw the pail, I laughed. It reminded me that Miss Lydia had a real sense of humor, if you just took the time to figure her out. When I first began studying dance in her underground studio, she was an enigma. Hair dyed red, lipstick bright red to match. White makeup that gave her the look of a geisha girl. A too-heavy figure, full-bosomed, her pink leotard revealing the rolls of flesh that circled her waistline, her pale blue tights clinging to legs that tapered from muscular, fleshy thighs to thin, shapely ankles.

She'd put a 78 on her little turquoise record player and start counting: one, two, three, four—waiting for our scraggly group to line up at the barre. I did my best to avoid being too close to her—fussing with the strings on my pink ballet slippers until I was sure that I could take a place toward the back.

We all knew Miss Lydia's story. She was a real dancer, not just another local enthusiast who had studied dance for years but never performed professionally. No, Miss Lydia had actually danced on stage with a famous company in New York City. Everyone in the class had memorized the details of her career. We had no choice.

"When I was chosen to join the Dance Ensemble of Brooklyn, I competed against 50 other girls," she boasted at the beginning of every fall class. She wanted to make sure that we understood who she was and what she expected of us. This was not just another basement dance class. We were studying with a great dancer. Over the next few months, she'd tell us about her teachers, Madame DePousier, who rapped her ankles with a wooden ruler, and Monsieur Deupres, who was a little too friendly, choosing to pat her derriere when he brushed by her.

There was no point protesting these abuses. Speaking up would have been understood as complete and utter defiance and resulted in expulsion from the class. So, knowing that it was good for her, she endured these affronts. When she hit our ankles with her pointer, we were to remember that it was good for us, too.

I first began to study dance with Miss Lydia a year after I took over as the manager of the skeeball arcade. I had last studied ballet when I was 12 years old and loved it. The thought of pulling in my stomach muscles and turning my ankles out appealed to me. But where in this boardwalk town, where people understood dance as jitterbug, would I ever find a proper dance studio?

On a cold October morning, after a long walk on the beach, I marched down State Street on my way to the arcade. Three teenage girls, their ballet slippers hanging from their shoulders, were coming out of the side door of a basement apartment of a tan stucco house. A black sign with square gold letters read: MISS LYDIA'S DANCE STUDIO. Tap and Ballet Classes Taught by a Professional.

I knocked on the door—only to hear a voice call, "C'mon in. What did you forget?" And there she was, Miss Lydia in her leotard.

"Who are you?" she asked me.

"Beverly Bridges," I said. "Beverly Bridges—that's my stage name. But I was born Norma Beverly Bluestein. Nobody has ever called me Norma."

I reached out to shake her hand. Her skin surprised me with its softness— it was like the exquisite smoothness of a newborn baby. Her hands could never have washed greasy dishes or scrubbed scuffed linoleum floors. I looked down at mine—bruised and battered by my efforts to rid the arcade of mildew, my skin speckled with splinters, sand trapped under my fingernails. Just hopeless.

She stared at me—her blue eyes, wide and bold. "Where did you dance?"

"Never danced," I said. "But I did sing professionally. Always wanted to dance though—I studied ballet for years when I was a kid. I had the lead in The Nutcracker at P.S. 147."

Lydia laughed, a great big rollicking laugh that shook her belly. It was a laugh that said, come on in, you're welcome, I like you. Here was a kindred spirit—twirling, tapping, and kicking her way through life.

"I'd like to study ballet with you," I said. "I know that I'm not Pavlova and that it's already too late for me to pirouette under the lights."

Lydia nodded. She understood. "You can join the Wednesday night class," she said. "You will be number six. We meet at 8:00 PM. It's $3.00 a session."

Lydia was a businesswoman. I could see that. There was not going to be any bargaining here. If I wanted a professional instructor, I'd have to pay for it. I was in my 30's, much too old for a dancer. My arms would flap in the air, like a tired seagull, paralyzed by a strong draft of wind blowing off the ocean, grey head alert, white wings beating furiously. Dancers were at their peak at 18 or 20: at 32, I was more like an aging swan, my silky feathers curled and knotted, in need of a regimen of pliés at the barre and jetés across the wooden floor to come to life.

"Worth every penny," I said, giving her a nod of respect. "See you Wednesday."

On the street, I found myself whistling the opening music to Swan Lake. I felt joyful and alive. Where had I hidden the black leotard and pink tights and the pink ballet slippers with the elastic straps that I had so meticulously sewn in place? I had bought them ten years earlier, thinking that I would once again study ballet. For years, they lurked in the back of my sock drawer, scrunched in a corner, collecting lint. Then, convinced that I would never dance again, I had moved them somewhere more remote.

I found them that evening in a carton that held my high school diploma and photos of me in oversized, jeweled sunglasses on the beach at Coney Island. The leotard had a few yellow spots on the front—a sure sign that I had worn it one day when I was eating a hot dog with mustard. I put on the leotard and stood in front of the mirror, surveying my body. It was a little tired and definitely middle-aged. The leotard and tights worked miracles, covering the stretch marks on my stomach and the beginnings of varicose veins on my thighs and calves.

And so I became one of Miss Lydia's regulars—arriving at her studio just before 8:00 PM after I turned over the arcade to Carol my neighbor across the hall, who had eyes like a hawk, and who always knew when Arnold spent the night over at my place.

"Break a leg," Carol would say to me, as I grabbed my coat and ran out the door. She was a big fan of Hollywood and she had a gold framed autographed photo of Rita Hayworth standing on her bedroom nightstand. "Break a leg."

There were six dancers in the Wednesday night class. The star was Roberta, who stood five feet ten inches, her long legs meeting her short torso. Roberta worked for Betty in the greyhound arcade, handing out an exotic array of plush prizes—pink giraffes that stood two-and-one-half feet tall, yellow lions that sported manes of orange wool—to winners whose dogs hit the finish line and rang the bell first. She had a booming voice and when she called the race, barking into the mike, I could hear her voice echoing in the skeeball parlor, four arcades away: "Here comes number one," she'd scream, "He's moving up from behind, chasing the tail of number three. Looks like a photo finish, folks. Here's the bell. It's number three!"

The crowd would applaud and whistle loudly. The winner would claim his prize. Then, Roberta would start again, warming up the crowd for the next race.

"Who is ready to be the next winner?" she called.

Roberta had studied ballet all of her life and you could tell that she was a frustrated dancer. She should have been on the stage, she would tell me, over and over again, as we adjusted our slippers before class.

"My legs are longer than those hounds'," she'd laugh, "and I'm more graceful, too."

Since we were arranged according to our height, Roberta stood at the end of the line, her jet black hair piled high on her head. When Miss Lydia began counting to the music—"and a one, and a two, and a three," Roberta would tilt her chin, and assume third position.

We followed after her, moving our legs tentatively. We were eager to earn Miss Lydia's approval. At five feet four inches, I stood fourth in the line, in between Gladys, who was a seamstress at the tailor shop on 5th Street, and Myrna, who worked in the drug store behind the prescription counter. Neither had any talent.

Occasionally, Arnold would stop by to pick me up. He knew better than to interrupt class and would stand outside, waiting for someone to leave before knocking on the door. Arnold hated ballet. He was a great fan of tap and ballroom dancing. The Charleston was his favorite. He loved Monkey Knees, where with both hands on your knees, you would bring your knees together, then switch hands to the other knees, then open and close your knees again, switching your hands back to the first knee in the finale. Arnold won a gold monkey on a chain, first prize in a Monkey Knees contest. Ballet, on the other hand, bored Arnold. It put him to sleep. He slept through our dance recital in December, waking to give me a big wink and to applaud the dancers in their purple tutus.

After the show, the entire company walked to the ice cream parlor by the boardwalk and ordered the kitchen sink—which had 28 different flavors of ice cream, smothered with whipped cream and maraschino cherries. Arnold tagged along, armed with his Brownie camera. Miss Lydia would give us a blow-by-blow account of our performance as she dug her long spoon into a mound of pistachio ice cream.

"Your last arabesque was a little crooked," she said to me, never looking up from the glass serving bowl that was contoured like a sink and was only missing the faucets. "If you arch your back, your leg will be straighter and higher." She was slurping the ice cream off a maraschino cherry as she spoke.

Arnold winked at me. He was just making sure that I could endure her post-performance rant. No one was ever perfect, except maybe Lydia. She was the lead dancer—the one who always won the best roles. She was the dancer who could be counted on to float across the stage without a misstep. Her pirouettes were perfect; her rond de jambs exquisite. When she finished her solo, the audience would stand up and applaud.

"It's talent and hard work," Lydia said, digging into another mound of ice cream, this time strawberry. For a moment, spoon in hand, Lydia stopped eating and looked at me. "You're not half-bad, Beverly," she said. That was as close as she could ever come to a compliment. Not Bad. Passable. The word good stuck to the roof of her mouth like a wad of chewing gum on the bottom of a schoolroom seat. Solid, hard, only a knife could scrape it loose.

I was loyal to her, despite her faint praise.

When Lydia said that she danced on the stage at the Cardinal Theatre, we believed her. She knew every inch of that space—the grey-green paint in the dressing rooms, the rose etchings on the mirrored top of the makeup table, the deep maroon of the striped velvet curtains. No one could invent those details. We imagined Lydia en pointe as the spotlight bounced off her purple tutu. Her fortes were brilliant. Her jetés exquisite. Miss Lydia, our Miss Lydia, was a ballerina of renown. How blessed we were to have her as our teacher.

Once or twice a year, Lydia would invite me to join her in the city at the ballet. We'd take the train to Manhattan for a Saturday matinee performance. From our perch in the balcony, Lydia would whisper her review to me as we watched the troupe perform. "Off-balance, that one," she said to me, as the woman to her right urged her to be quiet.

One Saturday, during the intermission, I returned from the ladies' room to find Lydia talking to a grey-haired man whom she introduced as Martin Peterson. "Martin and I have been friends for years," she said, her voice trembling. "We're both great lovers of ballet."

"Hi, I'm Beverly Bridges," I said, putting out my hand to shake his.

Peterson's handshake was firm. "I've thought of you often," he said to her. Then, turning to me, he said, "I could always depend on Lydia."

"Were you two dancing partners?" I asked.

Before Martin could answer, Lydia jumped in. "We were the best of friends," she said.

The house lights flickered and Lydia hurried me off, barely waving goodbye to him. During the act that followed, Lydia did not comment even once on any of the dancing. She sat silently, occasionally sighing deeply and dabbing her eyes with a white handkerchief. She dropped her program twice, the second time not even bothering to pick it up. After the performance, she walked out in front of me, her eyes darting from side to side.

"Are you looking for Martin?" I asked her.

"No," she said curtly.

After the performance, Lydia would usually give me a blow-by-blow critique of the dancing, lapsing into one story after another about her grand moments on stage: the packed houses, the crowd's enthusiastic applause, bouquet after bouquet of flowers. "Bravo! Bravo!" they shouted as she curtsied, over and over again.

This time, however, there were no stories. Lydia sat silently, looking out the dark train window. Her head was slumped against the frame and her body sagged.

"I never was a famous dancer," Lydia said to me, almost in a whisper.

She took out a large, white handkerchief and blew her nose.

"Those were all lies. I was just a back-up girl, filling in when someone got sick. Little bitsy roles, that's what I danced." Her voice was so soft now I could barely hear her.

"You want to know how I knew Martin. He was the stage director and I was his assistant. I was the seamstress who fixed broken straps, the brewer of the morning coffee. I ironed the costumes and redid the makeup."

The truth was pouring out of Lydia, word after miserable word. Lydia reached over and touched my hand. "It would break my heart," she said. "I'm telling you, Beverly, it would kill me. They look up to me. They idolize me."

When the train arrived at the station, Lydia was the first off. For a woman of grace, she stumbled on the last step, just managing to right herself. She reached out her hand to me. Her fingers were cold, like the feel of the nickels in the arcade cash register. Her breath was heavy and I could hear a wheezing sound as she inhaled and exhaled.

I pitied her. How had she managed to live with those lies? How had we all fallen for her stories? She was a fraud. A phony. All I'd have to do was to rat on her, tell Arnold and Jolly Trixie and the class.

"Give her a break," Arnold said the next day, as we marched along on the boardwalk. "We're all phonies. You're definitely not the hotshot singer that you claim to be. And I certainly never brought the house down as a comedian. We're all boardwalk blow-ups, balloons filled with hot air."

I pinched him to see if he would pop.

"Some balloons are tougher than others," he said, winking at me.

Arnold was a tough geezer, yes.

All week long, Lydia was on my mind. When I lay down in bed, she kept me awake. When I finally fell asleep, she was in my dreams, on stage in a white satin tutu, decorated with silver spangles. She was holding a bouquet of long-stemmed, red roses and curtsying under the spotlights. Just before I woke up, a young dancer snatched the roses from her. Lydia stood there completely stunned.

Our next class was Wednesday night. On Monday and Tuesday, I kept badgering Arnold.

"I'm under no obligation to keep her secret," I said to him.

"The only obligation you have is to take care of me," he laughed. Arnold just would not get into the discussion. It was my problem and he intended to keep it that way.

Part of me really wanted to expose Lydia. The other part already felt guilty. That would be a rotten thing to do—as rotten as fish guts stinking in newspaper.

After class, we sat in a circle and guzzled water. Lydia had been particularly hard on us—making us jeté across the floor over and over again until we got it right.

"Higher," she said. "Straighter. Extend your legs."

We were drenched with sweat.

"I read that the London Company's new production of Swan Lake will be opening next week," Susan said. She was the group organizer, always planning trips to the ballet.

Lydia was quiet. Everyone was waiting for her to begin one of her fabulous stories about her debut in Swan Lake, when the drunken conductor showed up fifteen minutes late and there was a major blizzard outside—with two feet of snow paralyzing transportation.

She was staring at me and I was staring back. She looked worn, tired, and afraid.

"C'mon, Lydia," I said, "We love that story. Tell us about your big debut, just one more time."

Lydia reached over and placed her hand over mine.

"It was during the BIG blizzard," she began.

Splinters

1970

FOR SOME TIME NOW, business has been awful in the arcade. Arnold says that it's bad at Playworld, too. We talk endlessly, not sure why things have soured. He thinks that people are tired of the same old place; that families with money are flying to Paris. It's hard to compete with croissants and the Eiffel Tower. I think he is wrong.

"The magic of the ocean never fades," I reminded him one July afternoon, when we sat on a bench in front of the skeeball arcade sharing a late breakfast of sesame seed bagels. I had parked myself nearby, just in case Joey needed help. He'd come home for the summer, with one more year to go before he graduated from Brooklyn College. Joey wanted to own his own business some day, just like Arnold.

It was hot, the fifth day in a row of 90-degree temperatures. Before us, on the white sand, two families were camped out, cooler chests plopped on their blankets, and green-striped umbrellas shading them from the brutal noon sun. The children were already whining for lunch.

"Paris is hot in the summer," I said. "The Parisians head south to Provence to swim in the Mediterranean. Why would Americans want to swelter in cramped Paris hotels, where the fans move the hot air from one side of the room to the other?" I had never been to Paris but I had read all about old people, abandoned by their children, who were trapped in their apartments and died from the heat.

"The boardwalk's passé," Arnold said, handing me my half of a buttered bagel. "It's old people promenading with their canes or limping along on their walkers. Sounds cruel, I know, but that's what I see." He spilled his coffee as he spoke, shifting his leg just in time. "Most of the time, grandparents bring kids to Playworld now," he said. "The old folks are full of memories—your father threw a fit when he rode in the bumper cars, your mother shrieked in fear when she was strapped in The Whip—but the grandkids don't seem very excited. The rides are small when compared to Disneyland. Imagine, ten million people visited there in their first ten years."

He was shaking his head at the number, which was probably double that by now.

"Wait 'til next year," he said. "Disney's opening Magic Kingdom in Orlando. We're small potatoes, fast becoming extinct. One day, like the dinosaurs, we'll be behind glass. Folks will pay five dollars to come to the Playworld museum to see the bumper cars and the roller coaster."

"Ridiculous," I said. The thought of extinction gave me hives. What would I ever do without my arcade? I swiveled my head and looked at Joey. He was polishing the glass counters that held the prizes. There were only two kids rolling the balls up the alleys. They were probably not even paying customers. Joey liked to give them free nickels just to make it look like we had some business.

"Last weekend was my worst ever," Arnold said. "I didn't even cover my expenses." He winced, as if suffering from a bad toothache. "Maybe it's time to cash out, to close up shop."

Arnold told me that Betty at the greyhound arcade was thinking of retiring. "I talked to her yesterday and she's fed up," he said. "By the time she pays her electric bill and her helper, and buys the prizes, she's in the red." Betty had been the boss of the greyhound arcade for 15 years. The thought of her giving up made me sad.

"Betty's a fighter," I said. "She would sink with her ship before she would ever abandon it. She loves life on the boardwalk as much as we do."

"Did," Arnold said. He lowered his jaw for emphasis. "I spoke to a real estate developer this week. You know how those guys always come by with offers. He wants to build condominiums on Playworld, ocean-front apartments with a big swimming pool. The idea is to trash the boardwalk arcades and go upscale and create Miami Beach north."

Arnold was sweating. I reached into my straw bag and handed him a Kleenex. What would we ever do with ourselves?

"We'd have money," Arnold said, reading my mind. "We could buy a trailer and travel cross country. I've always wanted to see the Grand Canyon."

I had never heard Arnold speak about heading west before. Arnold loved the ocean. The smell of low tide was perfume to him. He'd walk the beach with a plastic shopping bag gathering shells.

"Look at the purple in this shell," he'd say. "Incredible."

He'd pile the shells on the top of his living room bookcase, where they would remain in a heap, surrounded by a dusting of sand. Arnold wasn't very neat. He left it to me to straighten up when I slept over on Monday and Tuesday nights. That was a joke. I wasn't very neat either. I'd rather read a mystery than drag the vacuum around the apartment sucking in sand.

"I never really wanted to see the Grand Canyon," I said, tossing a piece of bagel to a sea gull that swooped down and devoured it. "Life magazine did a big story with color photos last year—so I guess you could say I've already seen it."

Arnold laughed. "Life takes pictures of the beach, too, but is that the same as walking along the water's edge in August, watching a man-of-war jellyfish float by."

I was afraid of those jellyfish and Arnold knew that. Once, when I was a teenager, I was fooling around with my friends and one of them pushed me backwards into the water. I landed on a man-of-war. I howled and I howled. "Cover yourself with wet sand," one of the old timers told me. The sand was cold and it did help, but the sting hurt for a long time.

"Pictures are just pictures," Arnold said.

"What would we do with money?" Doing without for so long had had its effect. I bought my clothes from the Salvation Army thrift shop, waiting for their post-Christmas sale to stuff a large paper bag for three dollars. I knew how to roll up five shirts, five pairs of pants, and five skirts and squeeze them into one bag. Sometimes, the clothes smelled like they had been lying in someone's basement for years. I would scoot over to the Laundromat and wash everything through two cycles, on hot. When my watch broke, I'd buy another at the flea market for two dollars.

"Money doesn't mean anything to me," I said. "If it did, I'd have left the boardwalk years ago. I've spent years counting nickels. $1,000 is 20,000 games of skeeball. I need $5,000—100,000 games—60,000 in the summer and 40,000 in the fall, winter, and spring—just to survive. 100,000 games to pay the rent and the phone bill and feed me."

"Just because you've always been poor," Arnold interrupted, "doesn't mean that you have to spend your entire life that way. What's wrong with money, anyway?"

He was trying to convince himself. I could hear it in his voice. Arnold hated presents. "Don't need anything," he'd say, turning up his nose at a warm sweater or a new pair of gloves. "My old ones have plenty of life in them." Then, he would show me his worn black leather gloves, which he had clumsily restitched.

I hid his frayed tweed cap once, hoping that he would think it lost. No such luck. He found it behind a box on the top shelf of his bedroom closet.

"How'd it ever get there?" he asked me, winking.

"Money can change your life for the good," Arnold insisted. "I've been looking at mobile homes, fancy ones, all fitted out with kitchens and bathrooms. We could drive anywhere in one of them. Miami, New Orleans, LA. All you have to do is let your finger land on a city and poof, you're there." His right forefinger landed on the bench with a thud.

When I was thirteen, one summer, we drove to Florida in the off-season, when my father said the hotels were cheapest. It was 90 degrees when we left New York City, heading down through Washington, D.C., Virginia, and the Carolinas. By the time we reached Georgia, it was nearly 100 degrees. We followed the back highways, riding up and down dirt roads that left our green Studebaker covered with a thick layer of red dirt. In the middle of nowhere, south of Atlanta, we stopped at Ma and Pa's Grocery for cold drinks and sandwiches. It was the first time that I ever saw a Colored Only sign, which was hanging on one nail over the side entrance. Under it, a black woman was smoking a cigarette. A small girl who was not wearing shoes stood next to her.

We walked in the front door and I fidgeted while my dad ordered three Cokes. Pa was behind the counter. He had a huge growth on his forehead and I could not take my eyes off of it. It was pink and bumpy and it looked like it was going to explode at any minute. My father squeezed my hand, to shake me out of my trance, but I stared at Pa, mesmerized. The thought of him slicing my sandwich roll made me sick.

"Florida doesn't appeal to me," I said. "Not sure about New Orleans, either. There are too many mosquitoes there and bugs love me." I swatted a beach fly as I spoke. "The breeze from the ocean blows the bugs away, but in the swamp they hover overhead and eat you up."

Bugs did not bother Arnold. Even a green-eyed horse fly like the one that I just swatted wouldn't dare approach him. One stern look from Arnold and they'd fly off in my direction. My olive skin was perfect for their stingers; my type A blood just what they wanted to drink. There was no such thing as a small bite for me. Within seconds, my arm or my leg or my cheek or my forehead would turn red and itch; within minutes, there would be a huge lump. Within hours, the bite would have become an infection.

We rarely spoke about money. We didn't need any to hang out on the benches on the boardwalk, drinking in the sunshine. The sun at the cabanas in the beach clubs wasn't any hotter. The sand there wasn't whiter, either. I didn't play canasta and Arnold didn't play poker. So, why would we ever want to belong to some fancy club where the cabana boys ran back and forth with trays of frothy rum drinks, topped by teeny pink and yellow umbrellas, stuck in a wedge of pineapple? I gave those umbrellas away to the kids at the arcade. They were made in Japan and, if you were careful, you could open one without snapping the toothpicks. I visited Gloria there once, at the Sunset Marquis where my beach chair reeked of coconut oil.

I reached for my can of soda, which was now warm and flat. "No one's approached me about buying the arcade," I said. "At least, not yet." I was 33 years old and I didn't have the faintest idea what I would do without my arcade. After Joanne's family vanished, when I was 16, I seem to have given up on my dreams. No one knew, of course. But I lived with such a heavy weight of guilt, having turned in my best friend and her family, that I shrunk into my own skin. I tried college for one year—because my father would never have forgiven me if I didn't. But I sat in the classroom and my mind wandered. I just couldn't concentrate. What should have been A's turned out to be C's and D's. I fought sleep when the professors lectured.

I had my little fling with show business, too, but never became a star. Beverly Bridges, my stage persona, just didn't cut it. Her jokes weren't funny enough and when she sang, she often slipped off key. So, Victor sent me to Sol and Sol left me the arcade in his will. That was 12 years ago. Where would I go if it closed down? What would I do without it?

Arnold patted me on the knee. I was pursing my lips, a sure sign that I was in distress. "Finding your path in life is a process," Arnold said, trying to be philosophical. "From birth to death, we search."

Those were strange words from a man who ran an amusement park. He was busy with greasing the gears and painting the cars of the wooden train that toot tooted around in a circle as the kids rang the bells. "Take me off, lift me up, slow down, speed up"—these were the rhythms of Arnold's life. Kids laughing. Kids crying. Smiles and tears.

Arnold wanted me to meet with Dave, the developer, too. "You have to look beyond his tie and his striped shirt and his slicked-back hair," Arnold said. "He's not the enemy."

"You never can tell who the enemy is," I said. I was thinking of my life as a spy, of me, goody-two-shoes Beverly, ratting on my best friend. I was worse than Dave, the man who wanted to tear down the boardwalk arcade and build condos. He was only a businessman, out to make money. I was a misguided kid, who ruined my friends' lives because I thought I was being patriotic.

"Let me call Dave and we can talk," Arnold said, massaging my sore left shoulder. For weeks I had had a pain there and I'd been trying desperately to learn to sleep on my right side. Change is difficult. How you sleep. What you do for a living. Where you live.

"Call, Dave, if you insist" I said, "but I don't want to sell the skeeball arcade. I'd kill myself before I did that." As a child, my mother always called me Sarah Bernhardt, referring to the French stage actress whose emotional style and famed death scenes earned her the title of the greatest actress of her day. "Dry up your tears and stop playing Sarah Bernhardt," she would say when I'd thrown a fit over an off-limits candy bar.

Arnold called Dave that afternoon and we met at the luncheonette. I arrived a half-hour late, dragging myself there after a sleepless night. I had counted sheep but kept forgetting what number I was up to. I had walked the beach searching for scallop shells. I slept fitfully, awaking once to remember a piece of a dream, me standing stage center in my sixth-grade graduation concert, singing soprano. That was before I betrayed Joanne and before I became Beverly Bridges.

Arnold and Dave were halfway through their breakfast of fried eggs, bacon, and toast, when I arrived. Dave was younger than I expected, perhaps in his late thirties. He reached out to shake my hand. There was a large yellow diamond ring on his pinky finger. His skin was smooth, almost hairless.

Spread out on the turquoise Formica table, before them, were Dave's plans for the new boardwalk. The skeeball arcade was gone, replaced by The Arcade, a six-story condo, with 60 feet of boardwalk frontage and the logo of a skeeball lane etched in its concrete facade. Next to it stood a new hotel, The Sea Breeze, its lobby a replica of the old penny arcade. Arnold's Playworld was gone, too. In its place, the designer had drawn The Boardwalk, a gated community of a dozen townhouses with an amoeba-shaped swimming pool set dead center, amidst artificially created dunes with beach grass. In one corner of the property, poised like an outdoor museum, stood The Whip, its spinning cars a reminder of Arnold's enterprise. There were benches and old-fashioned style gaslight lamps on the boardwalk

"Pretty cool," Arnold said to me, as I sat down and ordered black coffee. He wanted me to buy into this scheme. "Shows you what a little imagination can do."

I hated it. As far as I was concerned, there was no way I would sell out. What would I do with myself? Arnold was deceiving himself.

Dave handed me a sheet of paper. "The numbers," he said. "You'll love them. The magic number for Arnold was $750,000. I was being offered $300,000. I could do the math fast. I was being offered six million nickels for the skeeball arcade.

That's how I counted everything. My weekly food bill was 1,000 nickels a week; the monthly electric bill, 700. I had never calculated anything in millions of nickels before.

"That's not all," Dave said as I read the numbers. "I'm giving the two of you a percentage of the profits, ten percent for Arnold and five for you. You'll be earning a salary without working. Nothing's better than that." Dave paused to let us absorb the good news.

What did you do if you didn't work? I could just not imagine myself waking up in the morning with nothing to do. Traveling was fine but for only so long. I liked my own bed and my own pillow. A long weekend in the mountains was too much for me. After a day, all I could think about was the dust that was accumulating on top of the glass prize cabinets in the arcade.

"All you two have to do is sign and I'm ready to roll," Dave said, swiveling a ballpoint pen in his hand. "Your friend Betty's signed already. She knows a good deal when she sees one."

I shook my head. "Not going to sign," I said.

Arnold didn't look happy. "Beverly needs more time," he said. "Give us a week to think about it." Arnold was mopping the last piece of his toast in the runny egg yolk that remained. Dave's plate was already empty.

I sipped my coffee, which was cold now, as Dave rolled up the drawing.

"Don't wait too long to get back to me," he said, speaking to Arnold. He stood up, shook Arnold's hand, nodded at me and left. After he was gone, Arnold and I sat in silence. He was tapping his fork on the table top, a sure sign that something had unnerved him.

Finally, he spoke. "Dave's a good guy," Arnold said. "We're really being offered a sweet deal."

That was a funny word, sweet. Sweet was cotton candy, spun by the whirring machine in the booth on the boardwalk. Dave's deal was like sucking on a sourball.

"We don't have to give up," I said. "We can be the holdouts. Let Betty sell and everyone else too. When I die, I want my tombstone engraved, "Here lies Beverly Bridges, the Skeeball Lady.

"For God's sake, Beverly, stop being so melodramatic," Arnold said. "You're only 33! You've, we've got years ahead of us." He reached into his briefcase and pulled out a folded brochure.

"Look at this," he said, opening the brochure to a dog-eared page.

"That's the model, I want," Arnold said, pointing to a photo of an Airstream trailer. "It's 24 feet long with a queen-size bed, a shower and a porcelain toilet, and a full kitchen with a sink, fridge and gas cooker and hob."

Arnold had been tearing out Airstream ads for years from The Saturday Evening Post. He was in love with their shiny aluminum surface, and with their beautiful fittings: the silver-tinted windows and built-in wooden wardrobes. Over and over again, he traced endless journeys across the United States, blue lines north through North and South Dakota and down the coast from Washington State to the border with Mexico, red lines south to Alabama, Mississippi, and Louisiana. We would swim in the Pacific and in the Gulf of Mexico. Arnold knew the location of all the best campgrounds and of all the amusement parks, too.

"All we have to do is sell," he said. "The rest is easy. I'm 43 years old and it's time for me to break my routine. There has to be more to life than running Playworld."

"We just need a vacation," I said, although I didn't really believe my own words. "Two weeks away from here might just cure us."

Neither of us had ever taken a summer vacation. How could we? Summer was prime time. We never even ate lunch.

Arnold seemed intrigued by the idea of our running off for a summer vacation. "We could drive up to Maine. I've never been there. We might even visit my old friend Paul. He and his family spend a few weeks on Monhegan Island."

Arnold was smiling now. "We can put off making a decision on selling until the end of the summer," he said.

Arnold had a plan. George would run Playworld and Joey would manage the skeeball arcade. For years, George helped Arnold paint the rides every spring, bright blue on the wooden boats and a brash yellow and red on the airplanes. Known as the best auto mechanic in town, George helped Arnold grease the gears of the Ferris wheel and The Whip.

"Golden hands," that was how Arnold described his buddy George.

There was no doubt that Joey could handle skeeball.

"We can rent an Airstream," he said, breaking into a big smile. "I love this one with the mahogany paneling." He unfolded an ad, torn from a magazine, and spread it before me.

Just looking at the picture made me break out in a sweat. I was claustrophobic. Sleeping in a Girl Scout tent once made me so ill that I vomited for hours. Even a short ride in a crowded elevator gave me hives.

"I don't think I can do that," I said. "You know me and small spaces." I was waving my arms in the air to show him just how much I needed room.

"Don't be so melodramatic," Arnold said, lowering my arms to my side. For a moment, I had become Beverly Bridges, the actress, flapping my wings as I flew across the stage.

I was definitely not going anywhere. Not in a trailer. Not even in a car.

"Come up with another plan," I said. "This one won't do."

Arnold and I rarely fought. He was too nice and I was too passive. Even when I did get angry, it blew over quickly. He'd rub my sore shoulder. He'd cook me a cheese omelet. How could you stay mad at someone who scrubbed the frying pan till it shone?

But it felt as if we were on a verge of a fight. He wanted to go and I wanted to stay. We were at an impasse, like the Catholics and the Protestants in Ireland.

"See you later, Arnold," I said, desperate to escape. I needed to walk on the beach or take off my shoes and run in the water. Arnold did not respond. He sat silent and still.

I walked home, checking my mail before going upstairs. There was a crumpled envelope, postmarked from Andreas, PA. I did not recognize the handwriting but it was round, like a woman's. The back was sealed with a piece of scotch tape. I slit the top of the envelope and pulled out a single sheet of lined paper, folded in half. It was dated two weeks earlier. "Dear Beverly, I know that you will be shocked to receive this letter. For all you know, I am dead. I was always sorry that I, that we did not say goodbye. I live on a farm now. Call me. Love, Joanne." There was a phone number below her signature.

All of a sudden the saliva stuck in my throat, a thick pool of mucous that I could not swallow. For years, I had shut my mind to Joanne. When she vanished, I felt guilty for turning her family in. But I pushed the guilt away. At the Memorial Day parade on Main Street, I saluted the flag and sang The Star-Spangled Banner, my wavering alto voice louder than anyone else in the crowd. Patriots stood up tall and were proud. Patriots did their duty—no matter what the price was.

Why should I call her? I wanted to tear the letter up but I didn't, instead folding it carefully and slipping it into the zippered side compartment of my bag, in between my driver's license and two twenties.

I put on the kettle. Arnold wanted to leave Playworld, and Joanne had resurfaced. Chamomile tea—that was what I needed. I rummaged through the canister but there was only orange mint, much too sweet with a chemical taste, that Arnold once bought me in Atlantic City. Desperate, I poured the boiling water into my breakfast mug, the one with the pictures of two women and the words, "Smart Women Thirst for Knowledge." I had been drinking from that mug for years and it hadn't helped.

If I was a smart woman, would I be in this predicament now?

Were Joanne's parents still alive? What had she been doing all these years?

I picked up the phone and dialed her number. It rang three times before someone picked up.

"Hello," a woman said.

The voice was high—not the voice I remembered.

"I'm trying to reach Joanne," I said. "This is Beverly."

"I'll get her," the woman said. She did not recognize my name. In the background, I could hear a radio playing. Then, the woman's voice calling, "Joanne, it's for you."

The music stopped and news came on. There was an explosion at a local factory. Two workers had been injured.

"Beverly, it's you!" Joanne was on the line. "I knew that you would call."

Her voice was the same, low and definite, with the hint now of country—the Midwest perhaps. We had not spoken for 17 years. We were two teenage girls then, neighbors who lived houses apart in the West End. Two white stucco houses wedged on 30-by-60-foot plots of land. Sand on our front porches and in our beds.

"You have to come to see me," Joanne said, before I could speak. "We can't catch up on the telephone."

She didn't sound afraid but my first thought when she said those words was that perhaps her phone was tapped. The FBI might still be on her trail.

"It's a two-and-a-half hour bus ride from New York City," Joanne said. "I can meet you in Allentown."

She did not have to convince me to come. Joey could watch the Arcade. Arnold could wait. I called Arnold and told him that I was going out of town.

"Why?" Arnold asked.

"You won't believe this. To see Joanne." Arnold knew all about our friendship, although I had never told him or anyone else the whole story. She and her family had moved away suddenly—leaving everyone in the neighborhood puzzled.

"But what about our vacation?" he asked. There was sadness in his voice.

"It'll have to wait," I said. "She's invited me to visit her in Pennsylvania." I chose my words carefully, not wanting Arnold to tag along. But he didn't say another word. He could tell by the sound of my voice that I was going.

That night I had a terrible dream. Joanne was sitting on a cot in a prison cell, wearing a striped jumpsuit. Her face was drawn. The guard opened her door with a key and let me in.

"You have 30 minutes," he said.

When I entered, Joanne spat at me. It landed on the floor.

"You're a traitor," she said. "A turn-in-your-best-friend traitor."

"Get out of here," she said. She rang the buzzer for the guard and turned her head to the wall.

When I woke up, my nightgown was drenched with sweat and my back ached. It felt as if I had spent the night sleeping on a canvas prison cot. I was still determined to visit Joanne, but I felt afraid.

I made myself a cup of tea and called the bus company. There was a 12 noon bus on Friday to Allentown. Joanne, could pick me up at 2:30 PM when it arrived at the bus depot. For the next two days, I agonized about a present for Joanne. I was reading a new book about the history of the Communist Party in the United States but I did not dare bring her a copy. Buying her a piece of clothing was a bad idea. I had not seen her for years and I had no idea how big she was. When she was a teenager, she was as thin as or thinner than I—all ribs and legs with knobby knees. I could bring her a prize from the skeeball arcade—a set of carnival iced tea glasses or a china teapot from Japan. But I rejected the idea.

Then, I remembered how we would walk along the beach, swinging a plastic pail, searching for shells. We used to press the conches to our ears and listen to the strange echoes they made. Joanne said that she heard voices from the other side of the world. I would bring her a conch shell.

I saw Arnold later that evening. His shoulders seemed to be slumping more than ever and he swirled the straw in his coke, his eyes cast downward, avoiding my gaze. I knew that he was mad about our aborted vacation.

"It's not canceled," I said. "It's only postponed."

Arnold did not respond. When he got in one of these moods, I knew it was best to leave him alone. Eventually, he would creep out of it.

"Spoke to Dave this afternoon," Arnold said. "I told him that we were not ready. He won't wait forever, you know. We could be left out of the deal."

I shook my head. "No deal," I said. "Anyway, I'm off to see Joanne. All of this can wait."

Arnold went to his place, choosing not to sleep over. Neither of us was in the mood for sharing a bed.

"See you when I return," I said, leaning forward to give Arnold a kiss on his cheek. "Late Sunday night."

"Busy Sunday," Arnold said, without providing me with an explanation.

I made the bus to Allentown with fifteen minutes to spare. It was a hot, sticky day. The weather lady predicted that the temperature would be in the low 90s. I had traveled in on a train with no air conditioning. "Sorry, folks," the conductor's voice boomed over the loud speaker, "We've been trying to fix this for hours and we haven't succeeded."

Thankfully, the Allentown bus was cool and half empty. Who would want to go to Allentown, PA, on a sweltering summer day? In my bag was lunch— peanut butter and strawberry jam on white bread—Joanne's favorite. I made the sandwich just the way she used to, spreading a thin coating of chopped peanut butter on the bread, and then covering it with a thick layer of jam, and a sprinkling of coarse chopped peanuts. We had eaten hundreds of these sandwiches, laughing at the way the peanuts got caught between our front teeth. We would stand in front of the bathroom mirror, in her tiny bathroom, picking out the pieces. I did not want to think about my life as a spy.

I ate my lunch and fell asleep, waking to hear the driver announce that we were about to make a pit stop at Mary's Home Cooking, a diner 300 feet off the highway. "The rest rooms are clean," he said, "and the apple crumb cake is delicious."

Even if I was hungry, and I wasn't, I was much too excited to eat. Would I recognize Joanne? Would she recognize me? What did she know? What did I want to tell her? Part of me wanted to unburden myself—to confess. The other part was terrified.

I sat at the counter in Mary's and sipped a cup of coffee.

"Looks like you could use a slice of pie to cheer you up," the waitress said to me. Her name, Gretchen, was embroidered in red on her white uniform in neat stitches.

"Not hungry," I said.

"Where are you headed?" Gretchen asked me, determined to get me to loosen up.

"To see an old friend in Andreas."

Gretchen kept at me. "When did you last see him?"

"Her," I said, choosing not to answer the when question.

Gretchen frowned.

"High school friend?" she asked. You just could not keep this woman down.

"Sort of." My coffee was cold and the bus driver was signaling that it was time to board. I had spent years guarding this secret and I wasn't going to spill it now in a diner off Route 9.

For the remainder of the ride, I stared out the window and counted cows. I kept thinking about the story someone once told me, how teenagers played the prank of cow tipping, poking cows with a stick until they fell over. Thankfully, there was no one to bother me in the adjacent seat.

By the time I reached 73 cows, the driver announced that we would be arriving in Allentown in 10 minutes.

"Scenic Allentown coming up," he laughed. "Officially named in 1838, and known for its contribution to the local iron industry. When the railroad boom collapsed in the Panic of 1873, iron furnaces, big and small, closed. Allentown never fully recovered. Silk mills partially replaced the dying iron trade but the decline of manufacturing has taken its toll."

He had his speech memorized.

"If you are in town for a couple of days, walk through Old Allentown. Check out the Breinig and Bachman Building on the southeast corner of 6th and Hamilton. Built in 1894, animal heads were added to the building, which housed a men's clothing store on the ground floor. Some people say the heads were added to please one of the building's original tenants, a wholesale grain and animal feed dealer."

He did not say what kind of animal heads. I imagined wolves and foxes, sculpted out of terra cotta, their tongues hanging. The Allentown bus depot was deserted when we pulled in. Two old men were sleeping on a bench. The driver unloaded our luggage at the curb and pointed toward two swinging doors.

"That's the waiting room," he said, mopping his brow. "It's much cooler in there."

I decided to walk through the station and wait out front. Seconds after I arrived, a green Ford pick-up truck honked. The driver wore a white cap and glasses. The truck pulled over to the curb and the driver leaned over and opened the door.

"Hey, Beverly," Joanne said. "It's me."

Her face was thinner. There were cheekbones that I did not remember and a chin that came to a point. Her ash blonde hair was gone, replaced by a lackluster light brown. Her hair was pulled back in a ponytail, making the mole on her right cheek seem larger. Joanne used to spend hours making it vanish by covering it with makeup. She was wearing a T-shirt with the words Power to the People. For a moment, I thought that it was like the old days, some Communist slogan. But I noticed that there was a light bulb drawn on the shirt and below it The Pennsylvania Power and Light Company.

"Throw your suitcase in the back," she said.

The back was pretty dirty. The bottom was covered with straw and mud. There were two shopping bags full of groceries. At the top of one, there were three boxes of macaroni and cheese. The other was filled with beer.

I hopped up the step to the passenger seat and Joanne leaned over to kiss me. I turned my head to the side and her kiss, so tender, landed on my left cheek.

"I never thought I would see you," she said, as she revved the engine. "There are parts of your life that are lost forever."

"Didn't think I would ever see you, either," I said. My stomach was rumbling and I felt like I was going to throw up.

Joanne's fingernails were cut short and her hands looked like they were used to hard work. She was not wearing a wedding ring.

"So much has happened." She paused, as if to catch her breath. "My parents are both dead. My mother died of cancer four years ago. My father fell apart after she died. Three months ago, he put a revolver to his head and committed suicide. They had such a miserable life, you can't blame him."

She fell silent and we drove, across endless miles of rolling farmland, past one red barn after another.

"I still live in town," I said. "Two blocks from the boardwalk. I run the skeeball arcade and my boyfriend, Arnold, runs Playworld. My dad had a heart attack and he retired young. They live in Florida now in a tiny beach town on the west coast. I visit them every few months. My mom's bored but my dad spends all day fishing."

Joanne laughed.

"What's so funny?" I asked.

"Just the thought of your mother being bored. She was the perfect little housewife. My mom was a mess, remember? I couldn't bring anyone else home but you. The floors were filthy."

We were turning into a dirt road now.

"Two more miles," she said. "I live in a farmhouse built in 1880. It didn't have running water and electricity until we arrived in 1957. We bought the place from an old woman who was going into a nursing home. She was born in one of the bedrooms."

I could see the farmhouse now—painted grey with white trim. There were five or six white rocking chairs on the front porch.

"We're tree farmers," Joanne said. "We raise Christmas trees."

That was pretty ironic. The Jewish Commie spy family had ended up in rural Pennsylvania. Arthur, the lawyer with the straggly beard, raised Christmas trees for a living. Surely, the FBI could have found him if they had wanted to. No one had ever contacted me. They were gone and I was no longer a spy.

For years after Joanne left, I would walk by their house staring at the new people who lived there. The Gallaghers fit right into the neighborhood. They joined the church, and sent their kids (all five were boys) to the local Catholic school. Billie Gallagher was my age and he seemed to have a crush on me. When I'd walk by, he'd flirt.

"Come on, sit down," he said, gesturing toward the step next to him. "Would you like a lemonade?"

One day, he invited me inside. It was the first time that I was back in the house. Mary Gallagher had thrown out most of Joanne's family's furniture, abandoned in the house, with the exception of the dining room table, which was the perfect size for her brood. Cereal boxes, paper plates and juice glasses covered the table where I remembered the stacks of fliers for the marches in Union Square.

Billie shared Joanne's bedroom with his four brothers. It was wall-to-wall beds, a bunk bed and a trundle, with absolutely no floor space when the trundle bed was pulled out. The pine built-in closets remained. Joanne and I used to hide our treasures behind her socks on the third shelf, bright pink lipsticks from Woolworth's that we were both forbidden to wear.

"Not proper," said my father.

"Take off the red stuff," Arthur said.

Billie wasn't my type. He knew his baseball and his catechism. But that was about it. We never did date and I never visited the house again.

The truck stopped and we got out. Joanne unloaded my suitcase and the two bags of groceries and we headed up the stairs to the front door. A large white cat escaped as we entered.

"That's Marx," Joanne said. "Mom and dad named him. He's 15."

Marx did not look his age. His coat was fluffy. Someone took very good care of him.

"Leave your suitcase in the parlor," Joanne said, pointing to the room on the left. It had a fireplace and two beat-up flowered sofas. Between them was a blue-glass topped table, stacked with newspapers and magazines. There were built-in window seats and a library, housed in three bookcases, with glass doors, locks and keys. Joanne's parents' wedding portrait hung on one wall. I walked over to one of the bookcases, knelt down and read a few of the titles. They were familiar. I had flipped through these books before.

Joanne called me from the kitchen.

"I'm back here," she said. Her voice echoed through the long hallway. The kitchen was remodeled in 1957, Joanne told me, when they moved in. There was a yellow and red enamel-top table in the center of the room with six red and yellow plastic covered chrome chairs. There was a double sink and a fifties-style stove. The countertops were covered in yellow Formica and the floor had a diamond pattern of beige, yellow and red squares.

My mother would have loved this kitchen. I remembered her complaining about our grey counters. They were boring, she thought.

"This place is pretty dated," Joanne said. "I don't have the money to change it and I wouldn't anyway. It was my mother's dream kitchen. We laid the tiles on the floor together."

"Are you hungry?"

I shook my head no.

"Are you thirsty?"

No, again.

She poured herself a cold beer and sat down at the table.

"Do you know why I wrote you?"

Her question threw me.

"I'm not sure," I said.

"Because I owe you an explanation. We vanished in the middle of the night and you never knew why."

I was doing my best to look her straight in the face.

"We were in trouble. Big trouble. If we didn't clear out, we would have been arrested."

"Arrested?" I said, working hard to sound surprised.

"By the FBI. My dad was on their list. They followed him everywhere."

I could tell by her eyes that she was angry. "They followed him to work. They sat in cars outside our house. Everywhere we went, there were some guys watching our every move. This is supposed to be a free country but it isn't. That was what I loved about you, Beverly. You were my friend. Loyal, trusted. I never had to worry about you."

She paused to catch her breath. Her face was flushed. All that talk about the FBI and spies had taken its toll on her and on me, too.

"I always wanted to tell you everything but I couldn't. But you knew, didn't you?"

I tried to shake my head yes but it would not move—sideways or up and down. It was frozen in place. I was a rat.

"You knew about the rallies in the park. You met George and Eduardo."

"I liked Eduardo," I said, finally finding a few words.

"My dad was a good guy," Joanne said. "He believed in the rights of the working man. He hated that children went to sleep hungry. He wasn't the enemy. He was out to fix things. The FBI got it all wrong." She took a swig of beer and slammed the bottle on the table.

"I've never talked about this to anyone and I've always wanted to. That's why I wrote. You're the person from my past I can trust." She smiled at me—a wide, open smile.

"Best friends—that's what we were," I said, nearly choking on my words. I was thinking about my life after she left. My world had shrunk. How had a girl with dreams of a future—an international spy—ended up the manager of a skeeball arcade?

"I wanted to ask you more questions than I did," I said, after a few moments.

"Did you ever get the postcard I wrote you from Chicago? We hid out there for four months before settling on this farm. My parents would have killed me if they knew that I had written you. Everything happened so quickly. A phone call in the middle of the night from a friend telling us to flee, packing our bags, a late-night drive to a safe-house in Chicago."

"I still have your card," I said. I felt like crying now. I was on the verge of telling her, really I was, a long exhale, followed by an even longer confession.

"I knew more than you thought I did," I began, my left foot already starting to tremble. "I read those fliers about the marches in Union Square. Once, I saw a picture of your father at a rally."

"And…" Joanne said, "What did you think? Did you think he was a traitor?" She wasn't smiling now.

"I wasn't sure," I said. I had started to tell her the truth but I backtracked. Telling the truth was like pulling a huge splinter out of my heart. The splinter hurt, good God it hurt, but pulling it out meant sudden death. Extracting it would mean that the blood would gush forth, rupturing the main aorta. I would die before her, blood choking my words.

Some splinters are best left in. Those of us raised by the boardwalk know that. You pick away at them with a hot needle, you pull mercilessly at the end with tweezers, trying not to break it, and then, when all attempts have failed, you leave the broken piece inside—a dark spot festering.

"I was sure that you weren't traitors," I said, holding on to my splinter. It hurt but I was used to it now. "I envied you," I said. "Hanging out in your home made me happy."

Funny thing was, for once, I had told her the truth.

ACKNOWLEDGMENTS

This book evolved over a decade. I am grateful to many thoughtful readers who commented on individual stories: Bridgett Davis, Alice Gleason, Colum McCann and Lorrie Moore. Special thanks to Roberta Fiore and the Long Beach Historical Society in Long Beach, New York for sponsoring both a reading of "Jollie Trixie Keeps from Getting Blue" and a slide show of Dr. Kenneth S. Tydings' photographs. Thanks to Dr. Lawrence Tydings, for graciously providing me with his father's remarkable images. Thanks, also to Tahiti Starship for her elegant design, Licia Hurst for her careful editing, and Richard Edelman for his sensitive restoration of the photographs. Finally, let me express my gratitude to my friends and family for their support, encouragement and advice: Daniel Bernstein, Rory Bernstein, Bert Hansen, Lily Hoffman, Noah Shapiro, and Shael Shapiro.

SoHo, May 10, 2009

ROSLYN BERNSTEIN

Born in Brooklyn, Roslyn Bernstein moved to Long Beach, New York in 1948. She was raised in the West End of town, a short walking distance from the city's boardwalk, which runs for two miles along the ocean side of this barrier island. A poet and journalist, she has been a professor of Journalism and Creative Writing at Baruch College, CUNY, since 1974. Roslyn Bernstein earned a BA at Brandeis University and a MA and Ph.D. at New York University. She has served as the director of the Sidney Harman Writer-in-Residence Program at Baruch College since it was established in 1998.

KENNETH S. TYDINGS, POD. D

1917-1991

Dr. Kenneth Tydings and his family came to Long Beach, New York in 1945. He was the first podiatrist in that city. His avocation had always been photography. He authored approximately 75 instructional and photography books and filled those books with photographs of his family and his city.